"After being hurt during the earthquake…my face didn't heal right. It probably never will."

Frowning, Jay gazed at Kim with unseeing eyes. "What are you trying to tell me?"

"I'm ugly, Jay. That side of my face is—"

Jay framed her face between his big, gentle hands. His fingertips traced every bit of her face. Her eyebrows, the shape of her nose. The cheekbone that had been shattered and the one that was whole. His fingertips skimmed across her lips, following the outline and sketching the seam.

Kim stood immobile, afraid to breathe. A surge of adrenaline urged her to flee. But her body could only respond to Jay's tender touch.

"Kimberly Lydell, you listen to me." His rich baritone vibrated with conviction. "Even when my vision is twenty-twenty again, you'll still be the most beautiful woman in the world to me. That's how I'll always see you."

Dear Reader,

Welcome to another month of wonderful books from Harlequin American Romance. We've rounded up the best stories by your favorite authors for you to enjoy.

Bestselling author Judy Christenberry brings readers a new generation of her popular Randall family as she returns to her BRIDES FOR BROTHERS series. Sweet Elizabeth is about to marry another man, and rodeo star Toby Randall will let nothing stand in the way of him stopping her wedding. Don't miss *Randall Pride*.

An injured firefighter and the woman he rescued in an earthquake learn about the healing power of love in Charlotte Maclay's latest novel, *Bold and Brave-Hearted*. This is the first book of her exciting new miniseries MEN OF STATION SIX. In *Twins Times Two!* by Lisa Bingham, a single mom agrees to a marriage in name only to a handsome single dad in order to keep together their two sets of twins, who were separated at birth. And enemies are forced to become Mr. and Mrs. in *Court-Appointed Marriage* by Dianne Castell, part of Harlequin American Romance's theme promotion THE WAY WE MET...AND MARRIED.

Enjoy this month's offerings, and make sure to return each and every month to Harlequin American Romance!

Wishing you happy reading,

Melissa Jeglinski
Associate Senior Editor
Harlequin American Romance

BOLD AND BRAVE-HEARTED
Charlotte Maclay

TORONTO • NEW YORK • LONDON
AMSTERDAM • PARIS • SYDNEY • HAMBURG
STOCKHOLM • ATHENS • TOKYO • MILAN • MADRID
PRAGUE • WARSAW • BUDAPEST • AUCKLAND

Special thanks to the men of C-shift, Station 1, Torrance,
California. I owe you gallons of ice cream, gentlemen.

Added thanks go to Carolyn Greene and Linda Prine,
proud wives of men who wear a firefighter's uniform.

ISBN 0-373-16886-1

BOLD AND BRAVE-HEARTED

ABOUT THE AUTHOR

Charlotte Maclay can't resist a happy ending. That's why she's had so much fun writing more than twenty titles for Harlequin American Romance and Harlequin Love & Laughter, plus several Silhouette Romance books, as well. Particularly well-known for her volunteer efforts in her hometown of Torrance, California, Charlotte says her philosophy is that you should make a difference in your community. She and her husband have two married daughters and two grandchildren, whom they are occasionally allowed to baby-sit. She loves to hear from readers and can be reached at P.O. Box 505, Torrance, CA 90501.

Books by Charlotte Maclay

HARLEQUIN AMERICAN ROMANCE

*Caught with a Cowboy!
** Men of Station Six

Don't miss any of our special offers. Write to us at the following address for information on our newest releases.

Harlequin Reader Service
U.S.: 3010 Walden Ave., P.O. Box 1325, Buffalo, NY 14269
Canadian: P.O. Box 609, Fort Erie, Ont. L2A 5X3

Who's Who at Fire Station Six

Jay Tolliver—Dedicated to fighting fires, he doesn't need perfect vision when it comes to recognizing a beautiful woman.

Kimberly Lydell—Her life-changing scars can be healed only by a man who sees with his heart.

Harlan Gray—The dedicated fire chief will go the wall for his men; the only thing he can't do is escape a pursuing councilwoman.

Councilwoman Evie Anderson—Has her eye on the most eligible widower in town, Chief Gray.

Emma Jean Witowsky—The dispatcher has an uncanny way of predicting the future, especially when it comes to matters of the heart.

Tommy Tonka—An adolescent genius in all things mechanical, but he needs help from his firefighter friends when it comes to girls.

Mack Buttons—The station mascot, a five-year-old chocolate dalmatian who loves kids, people and the Men of Station Six.

Chapter One

The show must go on.

Those were the first words that popped into Kimberly Lydell's head when she felt the beginnings of the earthquake right through the seat of her panty hose. She'd been through plenty of California earthquakes and knew that's where you felt it first. In your butt, if you were sitting down. No big deal.

So she kept on reading the news report from the teleprompter as if nothing were wrong, looking straight into the camera, forcing an easy smile.

"In the Mideast, the prime minister of..."

She grabbed the studio set to steady herself as the vibrations of the earth escalated to an undulating roll. Overhead, the kleig lights began to swing in ever-increasing arcs. A roar like an approaching subway train resonated through the studio walls and shook the floor.

"...We seem to be experiencing..."

"Geez, let's get out of here!" Her co-anchor for the local six o'clock news kicked back the stool he was sitting on and made a dive for the far side of the room.

The cameraman and floor director headed for the exit, and in the control booth the show's director waved frantically at Kim to get off the set.

She got the message.

But trying to move was like fighting a riptide. The floor rose and fell in angry waves. The noise was ear-shattering. A camera fell over. A light crashed to the floor. The plywood desk where she'd been sitting offered no protection. Nowhere safe to duck, cover and hold.

Struggling like a drunken sailor, Kim got her legs tangled in her mike cord. She yanked herself free, only to trip over a cable in her now-frantic effort to escape. Panic clawed at her. She'd never been at the epicenter of an earthquake. Now she suspected she was. A big one.

In response to a high-pitched screeching sound, she looked up. The overhead light right above her had broken free. The screws pulled loose.

That was the last image she had before the room fell into total darkness. An agonizing pain sliced across the left side of her face. Screaming in terror, she fell to the floor. An instant later something impossibly heavy collapsed on her, pinning her legs. Dust filled her lungs.

And then there was only eerie silence followed by the sound of sirens.

THE FIRE ENGINE from Station Six roared to a stop outside the KPRX-TV building. Jay Tolliver hopped out as he had a hundred times before in response to fires, explosions and other disasters, man-made and otherwise. The earthquake had been a substantial one. He'd heard calls for help coming into dispatch from all over Paseo del Real, a moderate-size town in central California.

Their dispatcher, Emma Jean Witkowsky, had loudly announced between calls that she'd predicted this was earthquake weather. She hadn't, of course. But that never stopped her from claiming she had psychic powers—all due to her gypsy blood, she assured them.

A controlled surge of adrenaline shot through Jay as he pulled his helmet down tight. His job was to concentrate on this one building, saving lives and property where he could—the former more important than the latter.

In the cab of the truck, the fire station's mascot, Mack Buttons, a chocolate dalmatian, waited to see if he'd be called upon to calm traumatized children—or adults. Everyone at Station Six had a job to do.

The battalion chief was already at the scene shouting orders.

"Tolliver and Gables, we've got a partial collapse of the back third of the building and reports there are still victims inside. Do a preliminary search." He turned away quickly and ordered another pair of men into the neighboring building that had fared somewhat better, at least from outward appearances.

Jay snagged a fire ax and so did Mike Gables. Together they jogged toward the TV building's entrance. In the adjacent parking lot, car sirens set off by the earthquake screamed. Lights from emergency vehicles flashed red across the Spanish-style stucco building and the surrounding scaffolding that suggested the TV station had been in the process of remodeling— or maybe earthquake proofing.

Too little too late, Jay thought grimly.

He pushed through the front door into a lobby where only an emergency light shone from high up on the wall. The floor was covered with broken stucco and the furniture had been rearranged as though by some decorator gone mad.

Gables said, "Looks like KPRX evening news is off the air."

Flicking on his flashlight, Jay thought about Kimberly Lydell, the news anchor with the face of an angel and the smoky voice of a blues singer. He'd known her in high school but only from a distance. With a typical eighteen-year-old's raging libido, every time he'd heard her voice back then he'd gotten aroused. The past dozen years hadn't changed anything. Watching her on the tube was still an exercise in frustration—she'd gone from sixteen-year-old prom queen material to star quality.

He hoped to God she wasn't one of the victims trapped inside this old building.

They made their way along the hallway to the stairs.

"Anybody here?" Jay shouted, his voice muffled by the hard plastic shield in front of his face.

Cautiously they started up the stairs. Gables was a good partner to have. Experienced. Someone you felt safe with protecting your back.

On the second floor the debris was thicker, glass and plaster under their feet. A beam down. They'd passed the door to the first office when they heard a sound.

"I'll check it out," Gables said.

Jay kept going down the hallway. An electrical wire dangled from the ceiling, clicking a slow rhythm against the wall. No danger there unless they suddenly regained power. Then the wire would be hot and could start a fire.

"Help!"

He stopped in his tracks. The call had been weak. Female.

"Help me!" she cried again.

He followed the sound. "Keep talking, lady. I'll find you."

"In here."

Giving his shoulder to a jammed door, he pushed it open and swept the room with his flashlight. A broadcast studio, he realized, and his adrenaline kicked up a notch. Kimberly did the six o'clock local news. He ought to know. Like most of the men in Paseo del Real, he caught it as often as he could. The earthquake had struck at 6:14. It was probably 6:45 by now.

Whoever was here had been stuck for a half hour. Dangerous business.

The beam of his flashlight zeroed in on a woman

with collar-length blond hair. His gut clenching, he called on all of his professional training to keep calm. Not to race in there and make matters worse.

Pressing the talk key on the mike attached to his jacket, Jay said, "I've got a female victim on the second floor, third door on the right. I'm going in."

Gables's voice warned him to be careful. His male victim was conscious and Mike was moving him to safety. He'd be back.

"Please...I'm...hurt."

"Stay put. I'm on my way." Jay worked his way around toppled cameras and other debris. The roof had collapsed on the far side of the room, bringing down part of the ceiling with it. A wooden beam, one of those heavy Spanish-style numbers, had fallen into the middle of things. It'd be hell to drag out of there on his own and he saw immediately that the beam was resting right across her legs.

He knelt down next to her, forcing a calmness he'd been trained to communicate but one he wasn't feeling at all. "Hi. How're you doing?"

"Outside of being scared to death, you mean?"

He grinned behind his visor. One tough lady—

Then he noticed her bloody face. From what he could see, there were deep lacerations on her left cheek, her creamy complexion already showing signs of discoloration.

Pulling out a sterile compress stored in the lining of his hat for this very purpose, he fought a wave of nausea as he ripped open the package. Hell, he'd seen injured people before. Dead people, too. But not Kim—every man's dream woman.

"Looks like you're doing a little bleeding. Let me put this compress on your wound and then we'll see if we can get you out of here." He placed it on her cheek and she winced but didn't cry out. Tough. And brave. "Can you hold it in place for me?"

She nodded, watching his every move.

It didn't take Jay long to determine he'd need help to lift the beam off Kim's legs. He couldn't get enough leverage with his ax. Sitting back on his haunches, he keyed the microphone—

And that's when the second quake struck.

Instantly he grabbed his hat and placed it over Kim's head to protect her from falling debris. He covered the rest of her slender body with his own to shield her as best he could. She felt fragile and vulnerable as more stucco and plaster rained down and the building shook on its foundation. Wood splintered and metal groaned. Sirens wailed.

Finally the ground stopped shaking. But he didn't. A good, solid quake could give even a professional a bad case of the jitters.

"You still with me?" he asked, lifting the hat from her face.

"I wouldn't think of leaving the party early when it's as exciting as this." She gave him a tremulous half smile.

He chuckled.

Over his mike, Gables said, "Jay, you okay?"

"We're both enjoying the ride," he replied. "But

any time you can get us some help, I'm sure the lady would like to dance with somebody else for a while. She's pinned under a beam. I'm going to need a pry bar and some extra muscle. A paramedic would be helpful, too.''

''Gotcha. Unfortunately, that last roller knocked the staircase loose. It may be a while before we can get to you.''

Jay checked on Kim. She wasn't bleeding heavily but he was worried about her pinned legs. Loss of circulation could have serious effects. But he couldn't do much about that at the moment.

''We'll be here when you get here, buddy,'' he said into the mike. ''Just don't take a long lunch break, okay?''

''Understood.''

Looking up at him, Kim said, ''If there's another quake, this whole building could go down. Maybe you ought to—''

''I've got no plans to leave the dance without you, Kim. Just relax. My buddies will get us out of here.''

''You know my name?''

''Sure. Everybody in Paseo del Real knows you.''

A little frown tugged at her forehead, though it didn't appear to be because of pain. Probably experiencing some confusion from the trauma she'd experienced.

''Should I know you, too?''

''Probably not. But we did go to Paseo High together.''

She studied him a moment before her eyes widened—eyes the shade of the blue lupines that grew on the hillsides around Paseo del Real in spring. "Jay? Jay Tolliver?"

He grinned, pleased in spite of himself that she recognized him. "Guilty as charged."

"Oh, my gosh—" She winced, this time from pain.

"Easy, Kim. It's best if you lie still."

"I know…" Her battle not to panic was bright in her eyes along with the courage it took to stay calm. He held her hand and felt it tremble. "I remember you."

"I'm flattered."

"You shouldn't be—" She groaned and bit down hard on her lip.

"Let me see if I can get some of this weight off of you." Using his ax, he worked to wedge another piece of wood under the beam. Raising it only a fraction of an inch would help. But he couldn't get much leverage and the beam was damn heavy.

"Wait!"

Her cry stopped him.

"Why don't we just talk till someone comes? I mean—"

"Sure." Her lips had grown pale and that worried him. She was likely going into shock. Where the hell were his buddies? This woman was in deep trouble or would be soon enough if someone didn't get her out of here. "So what would you like to talk about?"

"You. I often wondered what had happened to you. How'd you get to be a fireman?"

"Firefighter. That's the politically correct term these days."

Her smile was weaker than before. "So?"

"I figured eventually I'd rescue some damsel in distress and she'd fall into my arms pledging her undying love."

"Count me in on that one, hero. What girl could resist?"

A lot of them, Jay suspected. Particularly those who knew his background—raised by a single mother on disability, the two of them living every day only inches away from disaster. A kid who had to work his way through high school, let alone community college, which he'd squeaked through during night classes, working extra jobs and trying to support his mother. Not exactly the kind of man who conjured up romantic dreams in the life of a high-school prom queen like Kimberly Lydell.

Damn, he'd wanted to know her so much better. But there hadn't been time. Not between his classes and two part-time jobs. Not when he knew damn well she was dating the most popular jocks on campus.

He shrugged off his memories. What he needed to do now was to keep her alive until help came. That would take all of his concentration. The only thing that mattered.

Adjusting his hat on her head to shield her from the plaster dust that continued to drizzle from the ceiling, he sat back.

"I don't think it's quite my size," she said as the visor virtually covered her eyes.

"Looks fetching though. Who knows, you could start a new fashion trend. You've always been the most stylish girl in town."

Hesitantly, she slid her free hand into his again, slender and delicate in his much larger palm. "Jay, how badly is my face cut? It feels…I need to know."

"Superficial." He wasn't a doctor but he suspected he'd just told her a lie. "You know head wounds bleed like hell and can hurt like crazy. You'll be fine."

She squeezed his hand tight, stronger than he had expected. "Thank you for being here."

"All in a day's work."

IT TOOK the urban rescue unit an hour to extricate Kim from the wreckage of the building. Jay held her hand the whole time; she wouldn't let him go until they lifted her into the ambulance.

Jay spent the night handling more calls because of the quake and couldn't get to the hospital until his shift ended at eight the next morning. Still grubby from work, he went directly to the nurses' station. His timing was perfect. The doctor was filling out Kim's chart.

"How is she, doc?" Jay asked.

Harry Plum, an old-timer in the community and everybody's favorite doctor, looked haggard. It had been a long night for the medics, too. "We're not releasing any information to the media yet."

"Doc, I was the one who found her in the building. I'd like to know."

He nodded. "She's in critical but stable condition."

"Her legs?"

"Not so bad—extended loss of circulation in her right leg, but we don't think she'll lose it. Lucky you fellows got her out of there as fast as you did."

That was a relief. "How 'bout her face? It didn't look good."

Plum turned his attention back to the chart. "Plastic surgery isn't my specialty." He shook his head. "I'm not optimistic. Some serious damage to her left cheek and the wound is ragged. They'll do their best, I'm sure."

Jay exhaled. He'd been afraid of that. "Any chance I can see her?"

"Not now. They're just taking her up to surgery. The OR has been going full blast all night."

The next day he tried to call Kim, but the telephone operator reported Miss Lydell wasn't accepting calls. No visitors either. He sent flowers and included his phone number on the card.

But he didn't hear back.

That was okay. She'd probably gotten hundreds of flowers from her fans. Jay was just another guy with a crush on her.

He didn't even mind the guys at the station razzing him about rescuing the prettiest woman in town, at least not much. He'd been doing his job. That's all any man could ask of himself.

And he'd do it all over again in a heartbeat if it meant keeping Kim Lydell safe.

KIM HAD STOPPED answering her door four months ago, right after she'd come home from the hospital. Isolated from the world, she'd been content with books to keep her company and her amateur efforts at sculpting clay to express her artistic nature. It wasn't that she was vain, although she'd always taken pride in her appearance.

Despite the doctor's best efforts, her scars hadn't healed properly. Her fair complexion meant every jagged line showed even with heavily applied makeup—which only made her look like a wax reproduction, as though one side of her face ought to belong to a macabre clown.

No, she didn't answer the door any longer.

Except whoever was out there now was damn persistent.

She slipped quietly to the window and eased back the curtain. The house she'd so proudly purchased when she'd first landed her job at KPRX-TV was small but secluded, perched on a hilly five acres covered with California live oaks. From her porch on a clear day she could see the sunset on the Pacific through a notch in the coastal range.

Unfortunately, a man now occupied that porch and he wasn't one to give up easily.

She sighed. From her days of reporting local news, she recognized Paseo del Real's fire chief, Harlan Gray. She couldn't ignore him.

Opening the door, she stood back so he couldn't see her clearly through the screen.

"Chief. What brings you out this way?" As far as

she knew, no wildfire was about to burn over the top of the ridge. And she'd cleared the brush from around her house per local regulations.

He took off his hat, revealing a head of almost white hair that he kept neatly cut in a butch. "Good morning, Miss Lydell, it's good to see you."

"Is it?" Not everyone would think it a pleasure to look at her these days; certainly looking in her own mirror was a less than pleasant experience.

"I wonder if I could come in?"

"I'm sorry, Chief. I'm afraid I don't entertain much these days."

"I see." Idly, he fingered his cap. "Well, then, did you happen to hear about the explosion at the plastics plant a few days ago?"

"I rarely watch the news any more." It was too much of a reminder of the career she'd strived so hard to achieve and then had lost.

"One of my finest men was injured in that explosion. He'd given his helmet to a victim he was trying to get safely out of the building and some glass containers blew up on his face."

"I'm sorry." She was. Truly. But she was barely coping with her own disfigurement. How could she possibly help—

"The young man was blinded—the glass cut the corneas of both his eyes. We think the blindness is temporary but the doctors can't be sure."

Blinded. Guilt gave her a sharp jab to her conscience. She'd been so devastated by her own problems, she sometimes forgot others were far worse off. "I am truly sorry, but I don't understand why—"

"The young man is Jay Tolliver. I think you may remember him."

It was almost as if the fire chief had struck her. The air left her lungs; her knees went suddenly weak. Fate had played an odd trick on her to have the boy—now a full-grown man—on whom she'd had a huge crush in high school be the one to rescue her after the earthquake. She'd known as an adolescent, as she knew now, it was not a relationship she'd ever be able to explore. Not because in the past she hadn't cared. But because he'd barely acknowledged her existence. And now it was too late.

When she didn't respond to the chief's revelation, he said, "Jay tends to be a little macho. He's out of the hospital but he won't let any of us help him. He's got this burr under his saddle that makes him want to be independent, even if it kills him. Almost literally. He's determined to do everything he's always done, despite the fact he can't see."

"I don't see how I could—"

"Miss Lydell, after the earthquake Jay talked about you for days—even when his buddies gave him a hard time about it. If he would accept help from anyone, it would be you."

Panic shot through her like a thousand-volt current. *She couldn't!* The fire chief was asking too much of her. For months she'd only gone out of the house to doctors' appointments and then only when wearing dark glasses and a scarf to cover as much of her face as possible. Not that the medical profession had done her much good. Everything else she needed, she ordered by phone to be delivered. As much as she might like to help Jay...

She began to tremble. Dear God, she couldn't! The thought of anyone seeing her. Pitying her. Or more likely being revolted by her appearance was too much to bear.

"I'm sorry...."

"He needs someone, Miss Lydell. I'm afraid—"

She shoved open the screen door and stepped out onto the porch. Into the afternoon sunlight. It took all of the courage she possessed to lift her face so the chief could get a good look. She had to make him understand so her own guilt wouldn't rest so heavily on her shoulders.

"Do you really think anyone who looks like I do could help anyone else?"

Unflinching, she waited while the chief studied her.

"He's blind, Miss Lydell." He spoke quietly, persuasively, as a father would. "I don't think he'll care."

Chapter Two

What in the name of heaven was the man doing?

Shortly after noon on the day of the chief's visit, Kim pulled her car up to the curb in front of Jay's house. It was a small wooden structure in a neighborhood of modest homes, each one featuring a porch with a swing perfect to enjoy on a warm summer evening. The front yard boasted a postage-stamp lawn, which Jay was now mowing.

Mowing with a power mower that was spewing exhaust and cut grass out the side.

Either Chief Gray was wrong about Jay being blind, or Jay was totally crazy. Not that he didn't look thoroughly macho in his cut-off jeans, his legs muscular and roughened by dark hair, and a cropped stenciled T-shirt that revealed a washboard stomach. Just the thought of running her palms over that hard expanse of abdomen made Kim shiver. The reflective dark glasses he wore and a few healing cuts on his cheeks took nothing away from the sexy image he created.

Her only regret might be that instead of wearing

his hair long enough to curl at his nape as he had in high school, he'd trimmed it far shorter, almost military in style. But definitely attractive.

Even in high school he'd held a special appeal for all the girls, dangerously so for Kim, who'd seen him as forbidden fruit—the bad boy who would be able to tempt her too much. Which hadn't stopped her from spending a good many hours fantasizing over the aloof adolescent who didn't seem to know she existed.

Some things never change, she thought as she adjusted the scarf she wore in public to hide the scarred side of her face. She got out of the car and slammed the door closed. With the mower roaring, he didn't hear her. She walked into the yard, the scent of freshly mowed grass ripe in the air, then winced as Jay proceeded to mow right on past his property line and across his neighbor's bed of yellow daffodils that under the warmth of the late February sun had just begun to bloom.

Two steps later, he turned the mower around and cut another swath back the way he'd come, clipping the flower bed again and leaving a narrow strip of uncut grass on his own lawn.

"Jay!" she shouted, jumping out of the way so he wouldn't mow her down, too.

Jay shoved the mower into neutral, stopped and listened. He'd heard something—or someone. God, how he hated the eye patches that covered both his eyes making him dependent on his other senses, the oppressive darkness of being blind making him less than a man. Vulnerable in ways he hadn't thought possible.

He tensed. "Is someone there?"

"Jay, it's me. Kim Lydell. Turn off the mower!"

The familiar smoky, blues-singer's voice of the TV newscaster sent a message directly to his groin. He killed the mower and turned his head in the direction he thought he'd heard her voice from.

"Kim? What are you doing here?" Over the years he'd had more than a few dreams about her, but never in the bright light of day—assuming he could have seen the sun, rather than simply feeling its warmth on his skin.

"At the moment I'm trying to save your neighbor's flower bed."

"Huh?"

"You managed to wipe out two big chunks of daffodils with that mower of yours. You want to try for some recently bedded pansies? The neighbor ought to love that."

Of all the things he'd dreamed of Kim saying if and when they met again, a discussion of flowers hadn't been the topic that came immediately to mind. "What are you talking about?"

"Jay, you mowed right on through the flower bed at the edge of property."

"No, I didn't. I paced off every foot of the grass before I began mowing. I wouldn't—"

She shoved a slick handful of leaves against his chest, and he caught a faint floral scent. It could have been Kim's sweet perfume, or the flowers she said he'd inadvertently trimmed. He wished it were the former.

"I messed up, huh?" he said. Worse than that, he'd done it in front of Kim Lydell, every guy's fantasy newscaster. For the past four days, since the explosion, he'd been desperately trying to act as though everything was normal. Dammit, his blindness was temporary! And if the lawn needed mowing, he was damn well going to—

"I hope you have an understanding neighbor."

"Yeah, probably." Clarence and Essie Smith were both in their eighties and kept trying to adopt him, particularly since the accident. There was yet another in a long line of casseroles molding in his refrigerator while Jay tried to relearn cooking for himself blindfolded. At least he was getting pretty good at scrambled eggs, the middles only a little runny and the edges singed. God knew what the stove top looked like though. "So, besides rescuing the local flora and fauna, what brings you to this part of town?"

"I never got around to thanking you for the flowers you sent to the hospital…or for rescuing me, for that matter."

He shrugged, wishing he could see her. But in his mind's eye he pictured her collar-length blond hair curving softly against her jaw and eyes that special shade of blue that reminded him of springtime wildflowers. "All in a day's work."

"The bouquet, too?"

"Yeah, well, I thought you might need a pick-me-up."

"I did, more than you could know." Her voice dipped to a low, husky note that was little more than a warm breath of air rippling across the hairs on his bare arms. "It was very sweet of you."

"How are you doing since Paseo del Real's little trembler?"

"Great, great. No problems at all."

He caught a touch of agitation in her voice as if she didn't want to talk about the earthquake and its aftermath. "So, I haven't seen you back on TV yet." Or in recent days, heard her, since he couldn't see a damn thing.

"I'm, um, on a bit of a sabbatical."

"Oh." He wondered what the hesitation in her voice meant.

"So, are you going to invite me in for a glass of ice tea, or something?" she asked.

"Tea?" His forehead pulled tight as he did a mental inventory of his pantry. "I've got beer." A beverage he could find in the dark.

"Even better."

She hooked her arm through his and he felt the soft swell of her breast brush against his skin. Heat simmered through him, making him ache for her. "Guess I can leave the rest of the mowing till later."

She laughed, warm and seductive. "I'm sure the neighbors will appreciate that."

Her shoes made clicking noises on the walkway. High heels, he concluded. And there was a subtle rustle of fabric with each step she took. A silk skirt, he thought. Or maybe soft cotton. His fingers itched to touch the material, to feel the texture and imagine the vivid color—cornflower blue to match her eyes or bright salmon to set off her honey-blond hair.

The perfume was hers, he decided, the scent lightly riding on each molecule of air he breathed, and he inhaled deeply.

He sensed by the slight lift of her arm when she reached the porch steps. A beat behind her, he followed her up the stairs without falling on his face— a significant accomplishment these days as attested to by the tender scrapes on his shins.

Thank God the doctor said the eye patches would go in three more weeks or so. By then he'd have bruises on top of his bruises. Meantime, he wasn't willing to sit around on his behind doing nothing. He wasn't going to be a cripple.

With a minimum of fumbling, he opened the screen door for Kim.

She stepped past Jay into the house, her eyes taking a moment to adjust from bright sunshine to the dimmer light of the living room. An overstuffed couch and chair, worn but comfortable-looking, faced a small fireplace flanked by a bookcase on one side and a big-screen TV on the other. Magazines were stacked neatly on a coffee table along with a remote tuner and a half-finished mug of coffee that looked like it had been forgotten or misplaced several days ago.

A big tiger-striped cat eyed Kim curiously from the center cushion of the couch then rose, stretched and yawned.

"Make yourself comfortable," Jay said. "I'll get the beer."

"Need some help?"

"Naw, I can manage." He walked through the arched doorway of the dining room, swerved to miss the chair at the end of the table only to bump into a second chair. He swore.

Kim winced. "You sure I can't—"

"Don't worry. I've got everything under control."

Kim got the distinct impression Jay was among the most stubborn men she'd ever met.

The cat eased off the couch, his bulk giving him the appearance of a yellow bowling ball with stubby legs, and followed Jay toward the kitchen.

Slipping her scarf off her head and looping it around her neck, Kim dropped her purse on the couch, deciding to follow the cat.

"What's your cat's name?"

"Cat." He opened the refrigerator, an older model, and unerringly took two bottles of beer from the top shelf.

"Cat? That's it?"

"He probably has another name but I don't know what it is. He was a stray that just sort of moved in on me and he didn't have a collar on or anything." Closing the refrigerator door with his elbow, he asked, "You want a glass?"

"No, the bottle's fine." There was already a collection of unwashed dishes on the tile counter and Kim didn't want to add to the clutter. "How long ago did he show up?"

"Oh, I don't know. Three or four years ago, I guess."

She stifled a laugh. "And you still just call him Cat?"

"That's what he answers to." He handed her the beer.

She took it firmly in her grasp so he'd know she had hold of it, and her fingers brushed his in the process. An electric warmth skittered up her arm in the instant before he released his grip.

"Thanks," she whispered, startled by the powerful sensation of such a brief contact. She wished she could see his eyes behind his glasses, the distinctive copper-brown she remembered so clearly. Unfathomable eyes that gave away nothing. "I was sorry to hear about your accident."

He paused in the middle of twisting the top off his beer. "A temporary problem. No big deal."

Assuming, according to Chief Gray, that Jay didn't manage to kill himself before he got his eyesight back. "I'm sure that's true."

He finished twisting the top off and took a swig. "I guess the explosion at the plastics company made the news, huh?"

"I wouldn't know. I haven't been watching TV much lately."

"Then how did you—"

"Your boss dropped by to see me. Chief Gray thought—"

"The chief? Geez, what is this? A sympathy visit?" He whirled, his demeanor angry, and he marched across the room to the counter. "I don't need your pity, Kim."

She could understand that. The thing Kim dreaded most was seeing pity and revulsion in someone's eyes when they saw her scars. "I dropped by to see if I could help you in some way, not to pity you." He was too virile, too much of a man, to be the object of anyone's pity, certainly not Kim's.

"I don't need your help, either. I'm getting along fine on my own, so you can finish your beer and be on your way."

"I see." She twisted off the bottle cap and took a sip. The cool liquid slid down her throat; his rejection left a bitter aftertaste.

In the silent kitchen, the cat nudged his empty dish with his nose, then padded across the room to wind his way between Jay's legs. Ignoring the cat, Jay stared at a spot a little to Kim's right, as if he didn't quite know where she was standing but didn't want to let on.

"I think your cat's hungry. His dish is empty."

"Right. I'll take care of it." Setting his beer on the counter, he opened a cupboard, and grabbed a box of Cheerios from a high shelf right next to a similar box of Friskies. Feeling his way with the toe of his tennis shoe, he found the cat's dish, bent over and filled it to overflowing.

Kim pulled her lip between her teeth. "Does your cat always eat breakfast food?"

"What?"

Sniffing disdainfully, Cat didn't appear impressed with the menu selection.

"You just filled his dish with Cheerios."

"I didn't—" He picked up one of the circles, smelled it and nibbled half. "He likes variety, okay?"

"The Friskies are in the box next to—"

"I know that. I got confused. It happens when you can't see anything."

Her heart ached for Jay, for his enormous pride that wouldn't allow him to bend, to accept anyone's help. "I did a story once at the Braille Institute in town. There are ways to organize your shelves and mark boxes and cans so you'll be able to tell which is which."

"That seems like a helluva lot of trouble when I'm going to get these damn patches off in three or four weeks."

"Patches?"

"Two of them." He lifted the reflective dark glasses, propping them on his forehead. "Great, aren't they? A real attractive addition to a man's wardrobe."

In spite of the pain she knew he was in emotionally and the fear of permanent blindness he must be experiencing, Kim smiled. "You look like some totally radical pirate. Very dashing."

She wasn't lying. With his burnished complexion, strong jaw and straight nose, he could easily be cast as a pirate hero in any Hollywood movie and scripted to steal a sweet damsel's heart. Not that she thought of herself as a damsel, of course, but the storyline had considerable appeal.

His full lips twitched with the hint of a smile, his mood switching back to the cheerful, determined man who'd been mowing his own yard—and making a hash of it. "You think so?"

"Absolutely. Very dangerous and very attractive."

"Maybe I ought to lose the glasses. I could start a new fad with the guys at the fire station. Everybody on the job could wear eye patches."

"That might be stretching it a little. Hard to drive those big fire trucks when you can't see where you're going."

"The more I think about it, the more I like it." Finding the cat's dish again, he carried it to the counter, dumped most of the contents in the sink— the rest spilled onto the counter—and refilled it with Friskies, returning the dish to its place on the floor. "How 'bout you give me a chance to change my shirt and pants, and I'll take you down to the station. We'll lay the idea on the—"

"No!" Panic shot through her. She didn't go out in public, not since the earthquake. Not unless she absolutely had to.

His eyebrows shot up. "What? You're not going to let me prove to you how well I'm getting along on my own? That doesn't seem very fair."

"It's not that." She couldn't bear the thought of the pitying looks strangers sent in her direction and their shock when they got a good look at her scars.

"Don't worry about a thing. I'll drive."

"You'll what?" she gasped. "You can't do that."

"Why not?"

"Jay, you're blind." And possibly a lunatic.

"So? Don't you remember that TV commercial where the blind guy was driving a classic convertible? If he can do it, so can I." He eased past her.

"He wasn't driving, Jay. He was being *towed!*"

"Come to think of it," he said as he sauntered down the hallway to what she took to be his bedroom, "I still could use some exercise. How 'bout we walk instead? It's only a couple of blocks."

She was so stunned by his offer to drive, Kim forgot she didn't want to go at all. Before she knew what was happening, he had changed into jeans and a clean shirt. He took her arm, giving her only an instant to wrap her scarf around her head and pick up the purse she'd dropped on the couch, and they were out the door walking toward the main thoroughfare running through Paseo del Real. His strides were long and confident, his attitude filled with bravado. Not unlike the way he'd been as an adolescent, she recalled.

When they were growing up, Paseo del Real had been a quiet college town with a permanent population of about thirty thousand. That number had doubled in the intervening years. Malls had replaced strip shopping centers; a second high school had been built at the north end of town. Industry in search of cheap land and the tourist business had added a new flavor and vibrancy to the community. Tracts of new homes blossomed on what used to be farmland on the outskirts of town, a more expensive crop than any farmer could afford.

At the end of the block, Jay stepped off the curb just as a car was turning into the street. The driver hit his horn hard and shouted an obscenity.

Kim yanked Jay back to the curb, virtually spinning him around.

Visibly shaken, Jay swore. "Where did that guy come from?"

"Around the corner. I didn't see him either." She'd been too involved in noting everything she could about Jay, the way his shoulders had grown broader over the years, that he'd added extra weight, all of which appeared to be muscle.

"Dammit all. I listen for crossing cars, not somebody making a turn. He sneaked up on me."

"Maybe you ought to be using a white cane so they'll watch out for you." At least the driver might not have sworn so loudly.

"Not a chance. I'm fine."

She gritted her teeth. Stubborn man. "How 'bout a Seeing Eye dog?"

"I'll put a harness on Cat, okay?" He turned, stepped off the curb and started off again. "Come on."

"Jay!"

He halted in the middle of the residential street. "What's wrong now?"

"If you're trying to get to Station Six, you're going the wrong way." She knew the main fire station was a block over on Paseo Boulevard and assumed that's where Jay had been heading—anything farther away and he might really have tried to drive her there.

He tilted his head, trying to get his bearings again. Damn, he'd really messed up this time and almost got Kim killed in the process.

Of all the people in the world, he hated the most for her to see him impaired. Blind. *Dependent* on the sympathy of others and their charity, like his mother had been.

That wasn't going to happen to him, not in this lifetime.

The chief should have minded his own damn business and not sent Kim around to "rescue" him. Instead, she was a woman he ought to be protecting. She barely came up to his chin, so slender he'd guess a good wind would blow her over, her hands delicate, small. Feminine. The kind of hands a man wanted to feel on him, all over him.

She wouldn't be interested in fulfilling that fantasy with any man who wasn't whole.

Standing stock-still, he listened carefully, hearing the street traffic on the main boulevard through town. Turning towards the sound, he felt the warmth of the afternoon sun on his back. This wasn't much different than finding his way out of a smoke-filled building, he told himself. You listen. Use all your senses.

He pointed in the direction he knew was north. "The main road's that way, right?"

"Yes," she said softly.

"Great. Then let's get going. I can't wait to have

the guys on C shift see me with the prettiest woman in town on my arm. They'll all want eye patches.''

KIM HAD NEVER thought of herself as a coward. She did now as they approached the fire station, and she pulled her scarf more securely around her head. More than anything, she wanted to turn and run away before anyone saw her.

But she owed Jay more than that. He'd stayed with her in a collapsing building when she'd needed him. She could do no less for him now. And whether he admitted it or not, he needed *someone*. Otherwise, his ridiculous macho determination was going to get him killed.

The three-story building was relatively new, its big doors mawing open to reveal two fire engines and a ladder truck gleaming red in the shadowed interior. One firefighter was polishing the headlights on the truck, another man was outside hoeing a recently planted bed of snapdragons, their colorful heads moving gently in a light breeze.

From the back of the station, a dog came trotting out. He stopped, cocked his head to one side, then whined, breaking into a full gallop right toward Jay.

Kim opened her mouth to warn him too late.

The dalmatian leaped onto his chest, nearly knocking him down, and licked his face like a kid with a brand-new sucker.

''Hey, Buttons.'' Jay laughed, scratching and petting the dalmatian as though they were old friends. ''I'm glad to see you too.''

"I gather you two know each other," Kim said dryly.

"Sure do." Jay give the dog another scratch behind the ears. "Kim, meet Mack Buttons, station mascot. Buttons, this is Kimberly Lydell. Be nice to her and she'll get you on her TV show, make you a star."

Planting himself right in front of Kim, his tail whipping back and forth, Buttons looked up expectantly with his big brown eyes.

Unable to resist, she petted his head, finding his spotted white coat like smooth velvet. The dog couldn't be blamed for not knowing she'd been off the air for months and there was little chance she'd make him or anyone else a star anytime soon.

"I've never seen a dalmatian with brown spots before," she said.

"They call this breed a chocolate dalmatian. But we figure somewhere along the way, he got into the wrong can of paint and now we can't get the brown out."

She laughed, and the dog gave her a tentative, well-behaved lick with his tongue. "Yes, Mr. Buttons, you're a good doggie, aren't you?"

When she looked up, they were surrounded by a half-dozen firefighters all in their neat blue uniforms. Instinctively, she turned her face to the side, trying to avoid their direct looks.

"We aren't usually that formal around here, calling the dog mister, I mean," one of them said, flashing her an easy smile. He extended his hand. "I'm Mike Gables, Jay's partner. He'd introduce us but he doesn't have very good manners. I'm the one with all the panache around here.''

''Watch out for him, Kim,'' Jay warned. ''He never has fewer than three women on the string at once, one for each day off during the week.''

''I see.'' In spite of herself, she smiled back at Gables, chancing a more direct look. She'd handled flirtatious men before. For the most part they were harmless—but not the kind of man she preferred. Tall, dark and a little aloof was more her style. Though in recent years she'd rarely had time to date, much less develop a relationship.

Two other men crowded forward to introduce themselves, Ben and Bill, equally good-looking but without the flirtatious glint in their eyes. She noted their curious looks, the way they checked out her scarf, but they didn't appear to dwell on what she was hiding. Maybe they didn't care.

They were quite solicitous of Jay, however. Eyeing him carefully. Asking how he was feeling. Any news from the doctor.

He shrugged off all their questions.

Another man who'd lingered at the back of the crowd finally spoke up. ''Are you going to give the lady a tour of the place, Tolliver, or let these guys keep on ogling your girl?''

''I'm not—'' she sputtered.

''Ignore Strong,'' Mike told her. ''Logan's just bucking for a promotion.''

''Are you guys *ogling*?'' Jay asked, his forehead furrowed in what had to be mock anger.

"Naw, not us," they chorused.

"We just don't know what a good-lookin' lady like Kim would be doing here with an ugly-butt guy like you," Mike said.

"Now just wait one darn minute." Kim drew herself up to her full five feet three inches, tickled in spite of herself at the way the firefighters kidded each other. "I'll have you know I've judged butt contests for KPRX-TV's day at the beach and Jay's would rate—" With an exaggerated effort, she took a look at Jay's rear end encased in tight fitting jeans. *Definitely a ten.* "At least a nine."

The guys hooted and hollered.

"Aw, come on," Jay complained, but he was grinning too, the squint lines at the corners of his eyes visible beneath his dark glasses. "Gimme at least a nine and a half."

"If you're very nice to me, maybe I'll let you appeal the ruling of the judges."

The entire conversation deteriorated from that point on. Keeping a straight face was next to impossible, Kim's self-consciousness about her scars slipping away under the sheer pressure of the firefighters' camaraderie.

And then suddenly, a high-pitched tone sounded, ear-splitting. Before it had stopped, the men standing around Kim scattered, running to their fire engines, slipping their feet into boots parked beside the trucks, pulling up heavy pants, hooking suspenders over their shoulders and grabbing turnout coats. Even the dog scampered off, leaping into the cab of one of the engines. It all happened like a well-choreographed ballet to the sound of a squawking radio that dispatched the helmeted dancers.

Jay took her arm. ''We need to get out of the way.''

He didn't hesitate but knew exactly the direction they should go to avoid being run over by the trucks that had already started their engines. They waited by a wall while the fire trucks rolled out of the station, one by one, sirens wailing.

When they were gone, Jay lowered his head. His shoulders shook and she saw his chin quiver. In a futile effort, he whipped off his glasses and wiped at his eyes, forgetting the patches were in the way.

''Jay?''

He shook his head.

''Let it out, Jay. It's okay.''

His Adam's apple bobbed as he tried to swallow. ''God, I miss that.''

Her heart aching for him, Kim did the only thing she knew how to do. There were no words to comfort Jay in his grief, so she simply took him in her arms and held him …as he had once held her when she was trapped beneath a pile of rubble. She hoped somehow she could give to him the strength and courage he had once shared with her.

Chapter Three

Jay stiffened and jerked back. Not that he didn't like having Kim's arms around him, her exquisite breasts pillowing against his chest, the floral scent of her hair tantalizing his senses.

He did.

But he hated like hell for her to see his weakness. To pity him.

Grasping her slender shoulders, he shifted her away, and immediately missed her closeness, the heat of her body blending with his. He shuddered as if a cold blast of air had swept between them.

"So," he said, trying to cover his sense of loss. "You want a tour of the place?"

"I don't want to be a bother."

He heard an unfamiliar chill in her voice—a voice normally so warm and arousing, sexy as hell—and he silently chided himself for hurting her feelings. The fact that he didn't want her help didn't make her offer any less generous.

"No bother," he said softly. "We're all pretty proud of the place."

"Fine then, if that's what you'd like to do."

Taking a moment to regain his bearings, mentally recalling where the door to the offices was located, trying not to make it obvious, he ran his hand along the wall until he came to the doorjamb. He shoved the door open and ushered her inside.

Except for the sound of the chief's secretary talking on the phone, the interior hallway was quiet now that the station was empty of firefighters. No laughing. No bantering voices. The things he loved most about being on the job.

"Where was the fire?" she asked, sliding her arm through his. "I couldn't understand what they were saying over the loudspeaker."

"An apartment fire on Toledo. Second floor."

"I hope it's not too bad."

"This time of day?" He shrugged. "Probably a grease fire in the kitchen." It was nights when things could get hairy, where fires burned undetected and were already out of control when the trucks arrived.

"Why did you decide to become a firefighter?" Kim asked.

"You mean besides wanting to rescue damsels in distress?"

"I suspect there's more to it than that."

He paused in the hallway to give her the easy answer, the one they used for school kids touring the station. "For the cheap thrills. Every time that tone sounds, you've got a chance for a trip to Six Flags."

"You're an adrenaline junkie?"

He couldn't leave it at that, letting Kim think he

was that shallow. "I grew up in the house where I'm living now. As a kid, every time I'd hear the fire trucks roll, I wanted to be there with them putting out fires, rescuing people, wearing that cool helmet. But the real question is why any sane person would stay on the job and risk his neck every day for strangers after you get past the adrenaline high and the excitement."

"And?"

He turned to her, picturing her blue-violet eyes looking at him, wishing he could touch her. Run his fingers through her hair. Weigh the silken blond strands in his palm.

"It's the brotherhood on the job. We may fight like brothers here at the station and give each other a hard time every chance we get, but we're there for each other when it counts." He rubbed his hand over his face, forgetting for the moment about the glasses and knocking them askew. He hadn't done a very good job of shaving that morning and there were patches of stubble on his jaw. He couldn't do anything about the press of tears at the back of his eyes, caught there behind those damn patches that kept him from being a whole man. "That's what I miss the most about being off the job. They need me and I can't be there for them."

"You will be, Jay. A few weeks, and then you'll be back on the job."

"Yeah." God, he hoped so. Otherwise he'd go crazy. He hated pretending everything was okay; hated swallowing the fear that rose up in the night to grab him. The dreams he was unable to halt, the explosion happening again and again.

Shaking off the feeling, he continued down the hallway, Kim at his side, her heels making those feminine clicking noises on the hardwood floor. Her scent faint. Seductive. Something that good dreams were made of.

"I've lost track of how many steps I've taken," he admitted, distracted by her nearness and his own fantasies. "The dispatch office—"

"Is right here. You want us to go in?"

"Yeah. No tour of the station is complete without meeting Emma Jean Witkowsky, our dispatcher and resident psychic."

"Psychic?" Kim frowned at the comment. "You mean she predicts fires before she gets a 911 call?"

"That's what she says…about two minutes after a call comes in. Says it's her gypsy blood."

Kim nodded, chuckling, though she wasn't sure she quite understood.

Jay shoved open the door marked Dispatch and Kim entered. Certainly the woman sitting in front of a U-shaped console of computer keyboards and screens could be a gypsy. Her dark hair was in wild disarray as though she had just finished a fiery dance to the music of violins and a concertina, and large silver hoops dangled from her ears.

"Hey, Jay, I knew you'd be coming in today. How are you, hon?"

Jay nudged Kim with his elbow. "*Now* she knows I was going to show up, but a half hour ago? Not likely.'' To the dispatcher he said, ''Doing fine, Emma Jean. I'd like you to meet Kim Lydell. I'm giving her a tour.''

''Hey, hon, I know you.'' Her dark eyes flashed with recognition. ''You're that TV person. Haven't seen you on the air for a while.''

Kim tensed, feeling the now-familiar self-consciousness wash over her when she met someone new. Automatically, she tugged her scarf more tightly around her face.

''I'm on a sabbatical.'' There wasn't much call for news anchors who look like macabre clowns.

The dispatcher gave her a closer look, her gaze uncomfortably penetrating. ''Don't worry about a thing, hon. I'm getting good vibes about your future.''

Although Kim wasn't a great believer in psychics, she said, ''Thanks. I'll hold that thought.''

''You do that, hon.''

Kim noticed a plate of what looked to be home-made oatmeal cookies covered with plastic wrap on the counter that separated the computer area from the rest of the room. ''Those look good. Are you the cookie maker?'' she asked Emma Jean.

''No, not me, but help yourself. Mrs. Anderson brought them over for the guys and they're going a little slow.''

''Thank you.'' Tempted, she reached for—

Blindly, Jay grabbed for her wrist just as her hand closed around a cookie. ''Don't touch those. They'll kill you.''

Her head snapped around. ''What?''

"Evie Anderson is the world's worst cook."

"The city councilwoman?"

"The same," Emma Jean said. "She's also got a mad crush on the chief. Thinks the way to his heart is through his stomach."

"A stomach *pump* is what you need when you eat any of her cooking."

"Oh, they can't be that bad." Gingerly, Kim bit off a tiny bite of the cookie she'd snatched, chewed and choked, desperately wishing she could spit it out. "Eeew, yuk."

"Told you so," Jay chided.

"She must have dumped a whole box of salt in there. They're terrible."

"She fell a couple of years ago and suffered a concussion," Jay explained. "I think she lost her sense of taste."

"But she's a very nice lady," Emma Jean said, defending the councilwoman. "And I predict—"

"Don't!" Jay held up his hand. "If the chief and that woman get together, there'll be mass resignations from the department. That's my prediction."

Kim couldn't help but laugh. Councilwoman Anderson was an attractive woman in her early sixties, practically an institution in Paseo del Real, if a little conservative for Kim's taste. She and the widowed fire chief would make a good-looking couple—assuming he had an iron stomach, she thought as she dropped the remains of the cookie in a nearby wastebasket.

"Say," Emma Jean said. "I bet you'd like to come

to the station's pancake breakfast this weekend.'' She whipped out a pre-printed pad of tickets. ''Only five bucks a crack. It's for a good cause.''

Kim glanced at Jay in the hope of an explanation.

''We're restoring a vintage fire truck to ride in the Founder's Day parade next September,'' he offered. ''Whoever sells the most tickets gets to drive. I figure I'm a shoo-in.''

''In that case, maybe I ought to buy my ticket from Emma Jean.''

''What kind of loyalty is that?'' he complained. ''Wasn't I the one who brought you to the dance?''

The dispatcher grinned at her. ''A girl after my own heart. Don't let these guys and their egos get ahead of you. How many, hon?'' She started tearing off tickets. ''You got a boyfriend you could bring? A good-lookin' brother about my age?''

Kim shook her head. ''Maybe my parents would come,'' she said impulsively. Both professors at the local university, they did try to support the community in a variety of ways. And even if they didn't want to come, Kim's investment wouldn't be large, only ten extra dollars....and it was for a good cause, as Emma Jean had said. That amount of money wasn't about to break her, particularly since KPRX was still paying her salary. Her boss, Alex Woodward, had told her to ''take all the time she needed'' for her recovery, although his generosity wasn't likely to last indefinitely.

She dug into the small purse she carried and passed over the money in exchange for three tickets.

A moment later, Emma Jean had to answer a call, so Kim and Jay excused themselves.

"Some friend you are," he grumbled, but she knew he was kidding.

Surreptitiously using his hand on the wall to guide him, he took her upstairs to the living quarters. Instead of a dormitory as she had expected, each firefighter had a separate bedroom that he shared with the men on alternate shifts, although each man had his own private locker. Then Jay demonstrated how to change the men's room into a women's restroom with the simple flip of the sign on the door.

"I think my preference would be for a lock," Kim said, a little suspiciously. "On the inside."

"We firefighters are the last true gentlemen in America," Jay assured her piously. "We'd never violate that sign. Unless we were invited to, of course. Or, in my case, if I didn't see the sign, which would be a darn good excuse."

She laughed. How he could joke about his blindness and at the same time be so stubborn about accepting help was beyond her.

They were in the third-floor TV room with its rows of recliners lined up in front of the big screen when the fire trucks returned. A loudspeaker announced, "Engine 61 in quarters."

"Let's go see how the guys did."

She followed Jay across the room where he opened what looked like a closet door. Her eyes widened. She screamed and snared him by his T-shirt, pulling him back. "That's not the way out."

"Sure it is."

"No, Jay! It's a big *hole!* You'll kill yourself." And this was a man who didn't think he needed help? She'd been right when she'd called him a lunatic.

"Not *hole,* sweetheart." He laughed. "It's our *pole.* Quickest way to get downstairs."

She peered past him. There was a pole in the center of the closet, all right, about six inches in diameter, but it looked like a hole to her—a deep one all the way from the third floor to the ground level.

"Come on," he said. "I'll slide down first, you follow me and I'll catch you."

She bristled. "I'm not going to do any such thing."

"What's the matter? Are you chicken?"

"Certainly not." Although she did have a certain fear of heights.

"You're not afraid I'll look up your skirt, are you? I promise I'll keep my eyes closed, if that's the problem."

She whacked him on the arm with the back of her hand. "It's just that I've…I've got heels on."

"I know. I've been listening to them when you walk." He waggled his eyebrows above his dark glasses. "Very sexy."

The heat of a blush rose up her neck. She hadn't been aware he was paying that much attention to the details about her, fully scrutinizing her in the same way she was noticing his attributes, all of them thoroughly masculine. And sexy. Like his full lips, especially when he was holding back a smile. *Kissable lips.*

"You get downstairs any way you like," she told him, whirling away from both Jay and her reckless thoughts. "I'm going to use the stairs."

His teasing laughter followed her out of the room as did his footsteps. She was intensely aware that he was "seeing" her in ways only a blind man could and very likely with more clarity than most sighted men would. She could only be grateful her disfigurement wasn't as apparent to him as the style of shoes she was wearing. Any man with reasonable vision would turn away from her, repelled by the scars that had healed so poorly.

At least any man she'd consider having an intimate relationship with—and that errant thought rocked her back on her mental heels.

THEY'D BROUGHT back the acrid smell of smoke to the firehouse and it hung in the air amid the sounds of his buddies checking out the equipment, readying everything for the next run they'd get.

Jay had never felt quite so left out, not even in high school when he hadn't had time to be a part of any clique. Or had the money to ask out the girl he wanted, he recalled, aware that Kim was standing beside him. What irony that she would be here now when he was in no position to do anything except enjoy the smoky sound of her voice and remember the face that had been a frequent visitor to his adolescent dreams.

The thing he hated the most—feared the most—his blindness, had brought her to him. Temporarily.

But it didn't change the fact that under other circumstances she'd be far out of his reach. Unattainable. And he'd still be one of the guys sitting in the stands, Kim his favorite fantasy.

He silently cursed the fact that though years had passed, their relative positions had remained pretty much the same—she was still the beauty queen, a local celebrity, and he was just a working stiff with ambitions above himself. A blind man who was only too likely to bash into a wall or trip over a crack in the sidewalk.

Buttons licked his hand in greeting, pulling Jay back to the action in the station house. In gratitude, he petted the dog and scratched him between the ears.

"How'd it go?" he called out to the men he couldn't see.

"Looked like the lady of the house was playing a little hanky-panky in the bedroom with her boyfriend," Gables replied. "She forgot about the lamb chops in the broiler and they turned into crispy critters with flames shooting up the vent."

"I figured it for a stove fire this time of day."

"Yep. Fun part was the lady's husband came home to check on what was happening. The boyfriend was hard-pressed to explain where he'd left his clothes."

"Oh, my," Kim gasped, a quick giggle escaping.

"Not a pretty sight," Gables added and the rest of the crew joined in with their laughter.

"Sometimes we need a degree in social work in addition to fire-suppression courses," Jay told Kim, still petting Buttons.

"Yes, I can see that." She touched his arm lightly, sending an arc of desire through him. "Look, I think I'd better be going. Would you walk me back to my car?"

For a panicky moment, he searched for an excuse to keep her around—a few minutes longer. An hour. He'd settle for whatever he could get. He didn't want her to leave. And he didn't have any right to ask her to stay.

"Hey, I've got a great idea," he said, knowing he was being a fool.

"Why does that make me feel like I ought to be running for cover?" Skepticism laced her voice as though she'd just announced some heavy-handed politician had promised never to take a campaign contribution from his favorite lobbying group.

"Kim, sweetheart, you've got to learn to be more trusting of men."

"Yeah, right."

"I just figured—since you were so worried about me—that you'd like to help me train Buttons to be my Seeing Eye dog."

"Your what?" she gasped.

"You were the one who suggested I get a dog. Buttons will be great, won't you fella?" With exaggerated affection, he scratched the dalmatian's coat.

"I thought you were going to harness your cat."

"I promise Cat won't feel displaced. I'll make it up to him by giving him some extra Cheerios in the morning."

Kim sputtered a laugh. The man was absolutely

impossible, and more than a little endearing. "Just how do you propose training Buttons to be your guide dog?"

"He's got a leash around here someplace." As if he could actually see, he glanced around the large garage that housed the fire trucks. "Hey, Gables, can you get me Buttons's leash?"

"Sure." Mike jogged to the back of the building and returned a moment later with a leather leash. "Here you go." He flashed Kim a questioning look.

She shrugged, mouthing, "Don't ask."

Jay bent down and snapped the leash onto Buttons's collar. "Okay, we'll think of this as a trial run. Buttons, heel."

The dog immediately complied with the order.

"Good dog." Jay grinned and rose to his feet. "Buttons, forward."

Jay and the dog began striding toward the open bay doors, and Kim was pushed to keep up with them, forced to hurry in her high heels. Darned if it didn't look like this experiment might—

"Jay, stop!"

He halted, turned back, frowning. "What's wrong now?"

She caught up with him. "I think it would be safer if you walked on the sidewalk instead of in the middle of the street."

"Good point." He didn't seem at all contrite about another near miss that had sent a passing car swerving around him. "Guess that's what happens when you're being led around by an amateur guide dog."

Not knowing whether to laugh or cry at the man's antics, she slipped her arm through his. "Until Buttons gets the hang of things, why don't we do this together?"

"Perfect," he murmured, and she wondered if the ridiculous idea of Buttons guiding him hadn't been a ploy to spend a little more time with her. Whatever the reason, he was a hard man to resist, particularly for a woman who hadn't yet gotten over her adolescent crush on him.

In spite of herself, a little thrill of feminine pleasure shot through her. Before the earthquake, a good many men had been interested in dating her. But most, it seemed, were attracted by her physical appearance, or by what they thought she could do for them in the entertainment business. Jay didn't have any such agenda.

The air had cooled considerably since the sun had slipped behind the coastal range of mountains, leaving Paseo del Real in shadows, and Kim shivered. She should have thought to bring a sweater with her.

"You cold?" he asked.

"Hmm, a little."

In an easy gesture, he looped his arm around her shoulders. Immediately she felt warmer, his touch rekindling a long-banked fire within her.

To casual passersby they'd appear to be a couple out taking their dog for an early-evening walk. Except Jay's dark glasses were neither a fashion statement nor an effort to shade his eyes. He couldn't see her, didn't know she'd changed from the woman he'd seen on television as well as the girl he remembered from high school. That she was now ugly, a woman few men would want to have on their arm.

If she didn't tell him that unpleasant truth, she was an impostor, a fake who didn't deserve to be in the same room with a man as courageous as Jay.

She stopped on the sidewalk. "There's something I have to tell you."

"Oh, damn, don't tell me Buttons has gotten us lost."

"No, we're on the right track. It's just that..."

"I knew it. I couldn't be that lucky. You've already got a boyfriend."

"No, not that either." She smiled, the movement of her lips tugging on the scar tissue that marred her face, and instinctively she ducked her head. "After the earthquake, the doctors did everything they could to rebuild the left side of my face. It didn't heal right. It probably never will."

Frowning, he gazed at her with unseeing eyes. "What are you trying to tell me?"

"I'm ugly, Jay. That side of my face is—"

He let go of the dog's leash and framed her face between his big, gentle hands. The scarf was in his way, so he carefully slid it back and then with his fingertips traced every bit of her face. Her eyebrows, the shape of her nose. The cheekbone that had been shattered and the one that was whole. His fingertips skimmed across her lips, following the outline and sketching the seam. With infinite care, he measured the shape of her jaw. And the dreadful, jagged scar.

Kim stood immobile. Afraid to breathe. Afraid of the revulsion she might see in his expression, hear in his voice. Her heart thudded painfully with that fear; a surge of adrenaline urged her to flee, to shut herself away again in total isolation. But her body could only respond to Jay's tender touch, thick ribbons of heat fluttering through her.

"Kimberly Lydell, you listen to me and you listen real good." His rich baritone vibrated with conviction. "Even when my vision is twenty-twenty again, you'll still be the most beautiful woman in the world to me. That's how I'll always see you."

Tears escaped to edge down her cheeks. She wanted to thank him but she didn't have the words to express the depth of feeling that filled her chest and tightened in her throat.

Her ego had been shattered along with her cheek, and whether it made her seem shallow or not, she'd needed to hear a man say she was beautiful—a man she cared about—even if his words were a lie.

Chapter Four

Jay treated himself to one last caress of her satiny cheek with the back of his hand. The loss of his eyesight had heightened his tactile senses. He relished the sensation of her smooth flesh, warm and vital, against his rougher skin. It hadn't occurred to Jay that she might need *him* instead of the other way around.

And, despite the courage she'd shown the night of the earthquake, the determination he'd seen in her blue eyes, she still did need him. Her tears proved that. And the gossamer bit of fabric—a scarf, he presumed—she'd been wearing to hide her face from others. Now he had to convince her she didn't have to hide from anyone.

"Hey, sweetheart, I've got another one of my great ideas."

She drew a shaky breath, audibly pulling herself together. "Spare me. Do you get these grand ideas often, or do you only hallucinate late in the day?"

"Think of yourself as my inspiration." Reaching down, he found Buttons and caught his leash. "There's a bar about a block from the fire station that's got the best beef dip sandwiches in the county. Let's have dinner there.''

"I don't think so, Jay...."

"You've gotta eat, don't you?"

"I don't go out in public much these days. My face—"

"But that's the beauty of the place. The bar's as dark as a tomb—which is probably why the beef dip tastes so good. God knows what kind of meat they're using." Taking her arm, he made a U-turn and headed back toward Paseo Boulevard. "Come on, Buttons. I'll buy you a hamburger without the bun."

"You don't like to take no for an answer, do you?" Kim complained as he ushered her along.

He smiled. Not when something important was involved.

KIM WASN'T at all sure going to dinner with Jay was a wise idea. Her nerves felt on edge, her emotions raw. After months of near-total isolation, she'd about used up her courage for meeting new people. Only the fact that the firefighters had been so unconcerned about her appearance gave her encouragement that she would survive a dinner in a dimly lit restaurant.

And Smoke Eaters Bar and Grill was dark, she discovered. About two-candle power and very intimate with small tables and cozy booths, few of them occupied at the moment. At the very back of the room was a pool table, a shaded hanging lamp illuminating the green felt, and on the wall there was a cork dart board with a bright red bull's-eye.

"Hey, there," the bartender shouted. "You can't bring a dog in here."

"It's okay, Curly," Jay replied, keeping Buttons on a short leash. "He's my Seeing Eye dog."

"You're putting me on. That's no guide dog. He's a *dalmatian!*"

Jay drew a sharp breath in mock surprise. "My God, I didn't know that! Thank heavens they didn't give me a dachshund!"

Kim nearly choked trying to swallow a laugh. Jay was totally outrageous and made her want to join in the fun. "According to section 1202 of the equal access statute," she told the bartender, "guide dogs have to be admitted anywhere the owner can legally be present."

Curly, who lacked even a single hair on his head, scowled at her.

"Is that true?" Jay asked under his breath.

"I have no idea if that's the right section of the law, but it sounds pretty good."

Jay barked a laugh. "Find us the best table in the house, sweetheart. We're going to have us some dinner."

TRYING TO AVOID curious looks from customers and employees alike, Kim selected an inconspicuous booth at the side of the room where the shadows were the deepest. She and Jay both ordered the beef dip sandwiches, and Jay covered his French fries with enough catsup to consider he'd had a full serving of vegetables with his meal. Kim opted for fresh fruit instead of fries.

They lingered over dinner, Buttons quietly curled up at Jay's feet. She discovered the bar was a favorite hangout of off-duty firefighters, Curly no stranger to Jay.

Looking very much at ease, as if he always wore dark glasses in a bar, Jay drained the last of his beer and leaned back against the cushions. For Kim, the reflective lenses were disconcerting at best. She wished she could see his eyes, though she recalled their copper-brown depths had rarely revealed what Jay was feeling.

"I've confessed all my dark secrets about why I became a firefighter," Jay said.

"*Dark* secrets?"

"Well, maybe not all the reasons," he admitted. "But it's your turn now. How'd you end up as a news anchor?"

Kim tensed. "Because I wasn't smart enough to be a mathematician."

"That's a pretty extreme range of occupations."

"And being in the broadcasting business is at the bottom of the range?" That's certainly how her parents viewed Kim's career. *Why can't you do something* meaningful *with your life, Kimberly? Not just entertain people over the supper table.*

"No, I didn't mean that." He leaned forward. "I meant for someone like you there had to be plenty of choices. You're smart. Beautiful. And have the world's sexiest voice."

She flushed at his compliment. "My parents are both tenured science professors at the university and my sister is getting her Ph.D. in some esoteric math modeling concept I can't even pronounce." Nor did she want to. "Don't misunderstand me. My parents love me well enough, I suppose, it's just that they don't particularly value anything that isn't pure science."

"So you're the black sheep of the family."

She nodded, then realized he couldn't see the gesture. "They don't seem to understand their precious science doesn't mean a thing except how it eventually affects people. I work hard...or I did before the earthquake...at making those connections for the viewers. Why a vaccine they're using in Botswana to eliminate mad cow disease affects our lives here in Paseo del Real. Or the impact a new child safety law has on children and their parents' pocketbooks."

Reaching across the table, he found her hand and covered it with his. His nails were neatly trimmed, his fingers long and tapered, his hand so large hers nearly vanished beneath it. Safely protected.

She'd feel that way if he held her. Melting into his big, strong body. Secure in the face of an unpredictable world. As she had four months ago on the most terrifying day of her life. A day that had rewritten her future in an ugly, painful scrawl.

He caressed his thumb along the length of hers. "You miss your job, too."

"Like being a firefighter for you, being a reporter or newscaster always fascinated me. Probably due to a misspent youth with too many hours in front the TV.'' She forced a laugh. ''I worked hard getting where I was—after college I started at a tiny station in northern California, sweeping out the studio because no one else would do it, writing copy for reporters who couldn't read above the third-grade level, reading everything I could find on international relations, finance, you name it. I was tickled pink coming home and getting the job at KPRX. Even my parents seemed marginally pleased with my success. But it was supposed to be a stepping stone to something bigger, eventually a network job. And now...''

''You'll have another chance. I know you will.''

She sighed, shocked by the vehemence of her own outburst. ''Sounds like you're trying to replace Emma Jean as the resident psychic.''

''No, I just know your voice can seriously turn a guy on when you're talking about the rise in interest rates.''

''I wh-what?'' she stammered, flustered by his comment...and secretly pleased.

''With your drive and ambition, nobody's going to keep you out of the broadcasting business for long. As far as I'm concerned, Barbara Walters couldn't handle being your understudy.''

''Goodness, but you're good for a woman's ego.'' Skilled at reawakening a woman's libido, too, telegraphing messages that sparked along nerve endings that had been dormant for a long time.

''Yeah, that's what all the girls say.'' Lifting her hand, he brushed a soft kiss to the back. ''Tell you what, while you're waiting to get the call from one of the networks, maybe you can help me out.''

She shivered, but this time it wasn't because of the cold. The ache she felt was of a far different sort. ''Of course, if I can.''

''You mentioned something about marking the canned goods in my pantry. I admit I am getting a little tired of dinner combinations like chili con carne and sweet peas.''

She wrinkled her nose, though she was pleased she'd worn him down enough that he'd ask for her help. ''I'll pick up one of those Dymo markers that makes raised labels at the store tomorrow and come by in the afternoon.''

''Great.''

The front door of the bar burst open and three tall, good-looking men in jeans and T-shirts sauntered in. Buttons stood, stretched and left Jay's side to trot over to greet them.

''I think we've been invaded by some firefighters,'' Kim said.

Just then one of the men petting Buttons spotted Jay. ''Hey, Tolliver, how's it going?''

''Is that you, Russ?''

''In the flesh.''

'''Bout time you guys from B shift showed up. I always said I could beat you at darts blindfolded.'' Jay started to slide out of the booth. ''Now's my chance.''

She snared his arm. ''Are you crazy, Jay? You can't play darts—''

"Sure I can, blue eyes. Just point me at the dart board and stand back."

His fire-fighting cohorts seemed to think being blind and playing darts was perfectly normal—even when Jay's darts missed the mark by three feet and they all claimed they had landed in the bull's-eye.

All Kim could do was watch in wonder at the depth of friendship and respect these men shared, and think about Jay calling her *blue eyes*. He couldn't see so he must have remembered—from the night of the earthquake? Or from longer ago than that?

Whatever the case, the husky sound of his voice calling her *blue eyes* had sent a ripple of longing speeding down her spine to curl through her midsection. Jay Tolliver was more potent now than he ever had been in high school and far more dangerous to a woman's heart.

THE DREAM started as it usually did—the tone propelling the members of C shift out of their beds, down the pole. A controlled surge of adrenaline pumping through Jay's body as he stepped into his boots and turnout pants, pulled up the suspenders.

This time he'd wake up in time, he told himself. There wouldn't be an explosion. The burst of glass wouldn't fly into his face, slice through his eyes.

All the engines had rolled, but Jay could only hear one siren—Engine 61—as they raced through the nearly empty streets of Paseo del Real. The plastics plant, the dispatcher had said. Toxic chemicals. The team that specialized in hazardous materials was en route.

Like a videotape on high speed, everything sped up. Smoke rising from the back of the plant. Flames licking the night sky. The battalion chief deploying his men. Jay ordered inside.

Wake up! God, he wanted to wake up!

He crawled on all fours through the smoke, moving so slowly it was as though he were caught in quick sand.

Run! Go back! It's going to explode!

A victim appeared out of the gloom, his eyes wide. ''Help!'' he silently mouthed over the roar of the flames.

I can't! It's going to explode!

The man held out his arms in a plea for help. Nearby, glass jars glowed red like giant candles—the devil's pulse. Sparks rained down from the roof. Frantic, the workman covered his head with his arms.

Don't give him your helmet. Not this time. Don't be a fool! Your own safety comes first!

Jay heard the pop of glass shattering, saw shards coming towards him. Individual pieces, like slow-motion darts, aimed at his face.

Duck! For God's sake, duck!

Crying out, Jay sat up in bed, his hands covering the patches on his eyes. Sweat dripped from his forehead, his body clammy with fear. His heart slammed against his ribs.

Why hadn't he ducked? For God's sake, why had he been so stupid?

THE NEXT AFTERNOON, the dream still haunting him, Jay paced the living-room floor, four steps from the couch to the TV, five steps from the wall to the hallway. In the kitchen he could hear Kim working, the clink of cans as she stacked and unstacked them.

A part of him wanted to lure her down the hall and into his bedroom with sweet words and hot kisses, make love to her there on the jumble of bedding he hadn't been able to sort out this morning.

But an emotion deeper than lust kept raising its ugly head. *Shame.*

Kim was doing for him things he couldn't do for himself. He couldn't read what it said on a damn can of sweet peas!

As much as he wanted to rationalize that *she* needed to help *him* to boost her spirits, *he* was the dependent one. She'd see that clearly now. No joke he could think up or stunt he could pull, like turning Buttons into a guide dog or playing darts blind, would provide a smoke screen thick enough to hide that truth.

As long as he was trapped in the black depths of his blindness, he couldn't pursue Kim.

He knew what it did to a person to be dependent on others, year after year, draining away their self-esteem, their desire to live. Being forced to rely on others for the simplest task. Begging for a few crumbs from bureaucrats to keep body and soul together. To clothe and feed a child.

Every day he'd watched his mother struggle because she was dependent on the whims of others.

Long ago he'd vowed he'd be self-reliant. Unless he could make that a reality again, he didn't have a right to claim any woman as his own.

Forcing his mired thoughts aside, he went into the kitchen, making his way to the refrigerator. "How's it going?"

Kim finished making the label with her Dymo marker and looked up at him. "Do you have any idea how many cans of chili con carne you have?"

He lifted his shoulders in an easy shrug, the fabric of his T-shirt straining across his broad chest. "It's an easy meal to fix."

"And catsup? You've got enough catsup and hot sauce to supply a restaurant."

"Wouldn't want to run out unexpectedly. You want a beer?"

"Sure." He twisted open the bottle and handed it to her.

"Thanks. I'm putting all the main-course kinds of canned goods on the second shelf, right at eye level. Chili, soups, corned beef. The vegetables—which are in short supply, I might add—are below that, along with the catsup. I'm not sure you're exactly getting a balanced diet."

"I get healthy stuff when it's Logan Strong's turn to cook. He's a real stickler for three squares a day with all the appropriate servings of fruit and veggies."

"Good for him." She picked up yet another can of chili, this one with a warning that it was extra spicy.

"I saw a bunch of scuba gear on the back porch. Do you do much diving?"

"Mike Gables owns a boat. When he's not squiring the ladies around, he takes some of us guys out to the channel islands. We do a little spearfishing, that sort of thing." He pulled out a chair and sat down at the kitchen table. "If you'd like, I'll get him to take us out on his next day off."

She sipped the beer and set it aside. "Not me, thanks. I'd probably drown."

"You don't like to swim?"

"Let's just say my childhood swimming lessons were a fiasco, with the teacher finally informing my parents I wasn't buoyant enough to go safely within twenty feet of the shallow end of the pool, forget any prospects for the U.S. Olympic team."

"That's a shame. It's real pretty under water. You'd like it."

"That's assuming I didn't sink to the bottom and stay there." She examined an open bag of noodles she'd found crammed at the back of the shelf. "I think your noodles are feeding a colony of little black bugs."

"Toss 'em. I didn't even know I still had noodles in there."

"Right." The bag under the sink was already overflowing. If nothing else, Kim's helping hand was cleaning out Jay's cupboard for him—and was making her feel ever so domestic. She probably ought to be doing the same thing at her house instead of hanging around with a man whose mere presence accelerated her heartbeat. "There are a lot of ropes on the porch, too. That's not scuba equipment, is it?"

"Nope. Rock climbing."

Kim shuddered. "You don't do anything easy, do you?"

"Hey, it's great fun. After you finish with the canned goods, you can drive me out to Joshua Tree and I'll let you lead me up some of those chimney rocks. The view from the top is terrific."

"Assuming I had enough arm strength to climb something like that—which I don't—I'd have to keep my eyes closed the whole time. I'm terrified of heights."

He frowned as he rolled the bottle of beer back and forth between his palms, and she realized her lack of athletic ability had disappointed him.

"What do you do for fun?" he asked.

"I read a lot. I just finished a biography of Saddam Hussein, which was fascinating. Really provided some insight about the strife in the Middle East."

"Seems to me the plot has to be pretty dull, just one war after another."

She marked a can of peas and placed it on the shelf next to some string beans. Beyond mutual physical attraction—which, for her part, was pretty sizzling— it didn't sound like she and Jay had much in common. Somehow she should have suspected that.

"I do a little sculpting, too," she said softly, confident that wouldn't strike a chord either.

"I don't know squat about art," he admitted.

She opened her mouth to offer to teach him the

basics but realized someone who went scuba diving and rock climbing was more into physical activities than cerebral ones. The exact opposite of her own inclinations.

Deep in her heart, the realization of their basic differences made her unreasonably sad.

She owed him her help until his vision was restored. After that they'd go their separate ways again, just as they had in high school. In the meantime, he was good to look at and fun to be with, not a bad combination for a woman to enjoy as long as it lasted.

Closing the cupboard door, she turned to Jay. "That's about all the arranging I can do with your canned goods. Would you like me to go through your closet and organize your shirts and pants by color?"

"What I'm wearing doesn't match?"

"White T-shirts are good." Very sexy the way it gloved his broad chest, showing off his pecs and flat stomach. "But it's possible you might want to wear something a little more formal from time to time. It would make things easier to find."

Taking a sip of beer, he appeared to give serious thought to her suggestion. "I suppose that would be one way to get you into my bedroom and from there we could—"

"I'm volunteering to arrange your clothes, that's all. Nothing extracurricular." She didn't dare imagine alternative activities in Jay's bedroom, not when they popped so easily to mind.

He gave her a wicked grin. "Darn, just my luck."

The moment she stepped into Jay's bedroom, she

had second thoughts about having volunteered for any project in such close proximity to his bed. The blankets were in a jumble, the sheets rumpled, making the king-size bed look like the scene of a wild orgy. She imagined all too clearly how an elementally physical man like Jay would create such chaos when he made love. There'd be no holding back. He'd give his all and the woman would have to respond with the same unbridled passion.

Her heart beating hard and her mouth gone suddenly dry, she dragged her gaze away from the bed. Was she even capable of the ardent response he'd demand? Would she be enough of a woman to satisfy his potently masculine needs? Dear heaven, how she'd like to find out!

Reaching blindly for the closet door, she pulled it open. To her surprise...and relief...she found Jay's clothes amazingly well organized. Shirts were neatly hung by color, working their way from a few dress white shirts through light yellow, brown and finally to shades of blue. His pants were equally well organized.

Even so, she couldn't quite resist touching the smooth fabric of his shirts, inhaling the scent of his fabric softener. On him, his masculine aroma blended with these lighter scents, making the combination uniquely his own, a union she was beginning to crave.

"You certainly don't need my help here. Your closet looks more organized than mine does."

"I let you look at mine. Maybe one day you'll let me look at yours."

His teasing double entendre slipped over her flesh with a feathery touch, chasing goose bumps down her spine.

"Don't count on it," she said, stepping quickly away from the closet and wishing she could as easily escape her own unruly thoughts.

Chapter Five

Saturday morning arrived bright and sunny, which did little to ease Kim's anxieties about attending the pancake breakfast at the fire station.

Perversely, she wanted to see Jay again but not at the cost of being gawked at by all manner of stangers. People who might well recognize her. Stare at her. *Pity* her.

Yet Jay was the one man she could be around without being self-conscious about her appearance. He made her feel feminine. Beautiful again. As unworthy as her need to feel attractive might be, her shattered ego longed for some semblance of normalcy.

Besides, she rationalized, if she—or someone— didn't watch out for Jay, who knew what kind of a crazy stunt he'd try next? What did it matter that they had little in common?

She arrived at the fire station to find cars crowding the parking lot and lining the street; more than a hundred people milled around in the early-morning chill, most carrying paper plates stacked with pancakes. There were families with children of all ages and proud parents sitting at rows of tables with their firefighter sons. The fire engines had been drawn out onto the driveway, leaving the huge garage empty for the festivities.

She almost lost her nerve. Her stomach knotted at the thought of facing half the town of Paseo del Real and her hands turned clammy. But before she could turn tail and run, one of Jay's buddies walked up to her.

"Hello, Kim, I'm glad you came." A tall man with sandy-brown hair, he spoke in a soft voice but one that carried a certain authority without being overbearing. "Jay's been looking for you."

Recognizing him from her prior visit to the station as the man who'd lingered in the background, she said, "You're Logan, aren't you?" The stickler for three squares a day.

"Logan Strong. I'm one of the ladder-truck crew." He looked pleased she'd remembered his name. "Jay's out checking on Big Red."

"Big Red?" she echoed.

"The fire truck we're restoring. It's a real classic. The city bought it in 1935, and it stayed in service till sometime in the sixties. They've housed it in the city yard since then."

"Oh, yes, the reason for the breakfast."

"Right." His smile softened the rugged lines of his face. "You want me to show you the way?"

A little panicked by the crowd, she glanced around in search of a graceful way to escape, keeping her head dipped to the side, her scarf securely in place.

''He'd be real disappointed if he didn't get a chance to say hello.''

Evidently Logan Strong was something of a mind reader, guessing that she wanted to flee. But leaving wasn't really an option. Not only had she promised Jay she'd be here, she'd sent tickets to her parents, too. They wouldn't understand if they showed up and didn't find Kim here.

Squaring her shoulders, she adjusted the scarf around her face again and forced a smile. ''Lead the way, Mr. Strong.''

The fire truck was parked near the training tower where firefighters learned to carry heavy lengths of hose up ladders and victims safely back down. The truck itself looked like it had come out of a Laurel and Hardy film, the driver exposed to the elements in an open cab, the firemen expected to hang onto the back as the truck raced through the city.

The motor had been pulled out of the truck and hung on an A-frame nearby. In fact, the entire inside of the engine compartment had been emptied and the truck was up on blocks, suggesting the restoration process had a long way to go.

Kim's heart stumbled when she spotted Jay standing beside the truck, his uniform perfectly tailored to fit his broad shoulders and lean hips. He looked capable and efficient, the press of his pants razor sharp. A stranger wouldn't suspect his dark glasses disguised a man who was blind.

Yet it was only because of his blindness that Kim felt free to be here with him. If he could see, she would never have had the courage to face him even with a scarf hiding most of her face. The fear of seeing pity and revulsion in his eyes would have kept her away.

"Hey, Tolliver," Logan said as they approached. "I found somebody you've been looking for."

"Hi, Jay," she said.

His quick smile spoke volumes about how glad he was that she had come. He reached out his hand to her. "Take a look at Big Red. Isn't she a beaut?"

"Yes," she said, though she wasn't thinking about the fire truck as, despite herself, she welcomed the warmth of his fingers closing around hers. "You look pretty sharp yourself, mister."

"I clean up good, huh?"

"The lipstick on your cheek is a particularly nice touch."

"What?" Embarrassed, he rubbed his hand across his face. "It had to be Mrs. Anderson. She gets a little gushy sometimes."

"I'm sure you have that effect on all the women."

"Usually just the ones over sixty and under age five."

Jay had that heady effect on her, too, creating an uncanny desire to kiss him, but Kim didn't think it wise to mention that small failing of hers.

"Where's your guide dog?" she asked in an effort to redirect her wayward thoughts.

"Mack Buttons is on duty entertaining the kids. They've got him around here somewhere."

She scanned the milling crowd until she spotted a

covey of youngsters, Buttons the center of their attention with one of the firefighters supervising. She laughed as a small child slipped the dog a bite of her pancake. "Looks like he's doing a good job but I don't think he's going to be hungry for dinner."

"Pancakes?"

"Probably as nutritious as Cheerios for your cat."

He gave an unconcerned shrug. "Say, I want you to meet our chief mechanic. You see a kid around here with spiky hair and pimples?"

The description was a perfect match for a slender adolescent who was diligently polishing the chrome on one of the headlights.

"Come here, Tommy," Jay called when Kim identified the youngster. "I want you to meet somebody."

Looking reluctant to be pulled away from his crucial task, he walked over to Jay, who introduced Tommy Tonka to Kim. The youngster's gaze flitted from Jay to Kim, held a moment of recognition, then darted back to Jay again.

"Tommy's a total genius when it comes to the inner workings of Big Red. He's practically in charge of overhauling the whole engine."

The boy blushed scarlet, and his gaze dropped to the ground, searching out an imaginary rock for his toe to shove around on the concrete. His tennis shoes were scuffed and holey, his laces untied. "I'm not that good," he mumbled.

Reaching out, Jay found the kid's shoulder and gave him an encouraging squeeze. "Yeah, you are that good, and we sure couldn't do this job without you.''

Kim was touched by the flash of pleasure in Tommy's eyes and how he quickly looked away again. *Shy* did not begin to describe the young man's personality yet she suspected the men of Station Six had found a way to reach him.

Jay talked to the boy for a while about guy things— starter motors and transmissions—then let the youngster go back to his solitary task by saying, ''I've got to see that Kim gets some pancakes before they're all gone. We'll talk later, okay?''

With a shy glance at Kim, Tommy escaped with his polishing cloth to the far side of the truck.

''The kid's a little bashful,'' Jay said after they'd walked away from the fire truck toward the tables set up to cook and serve breakfast.

''So I gathered.''

''Lots better than he used to be, though. Hardly would talk to any of us at first, just tinkered with the truck engine. Now we're working on getting him to talk to girls.''

''From what I've seen that may take a while.''

''We figure all we need is a girl who knows a wrench from a screwdriver and we'll be set. The kid really is a genius but he's kind of got tunnel vision.''

Kim could understand that. Her parents and sister were geniuses, too, and so focused on their own specialities they rarely had time or inclination to discuss anything else. Half the time they didn't even talk to each other.

"I'll keep an eye out for a girl with those qualifications," she promised.

Chief Gray was busily flipping pancakes while two firefighters with aprons tied around their waists were pouring orange juice and serving up little paper cups of maple syrup. Kim and Jay got in line.

"Maybe I should have volunteered to help cook," Jay said, his head close to hers.

"I imagine most of these people would appreciate not having their pancakes served up off the floor," she suggested mildly.

"You have a point. I'm better at darts, anyway."

Laughing, she nudged him with her elbow.

After a brief wait, Chief Gray slid a stack of pancakes on to Kim's paper plate. "Glad you could join us, Ms. Lydell."

"They tell me your pancakes are world-renowned."

"It's the real reason the city council promoted me to chief fifteen years ago. No one else in the station house could make a decent batch of pancakes." He gave her a friendly wink, then piled pancakes on Jay's plate, steadying it with his free hand. "Next year I expect you behind this table helping out, Tolliver. No slackers in my department."

"Yes, sir. I'll be here, sir."

Kim noticed, despite his jovial words, the chief's fatherly look of concern. She imagined the real reason Gray had been promoted was that he cared so much about the men and women in his department.

She guided Jay toward an empty table warmed by

the winter sun. The rays were not as powerful as this inland valley experienced during the summer months when the locals relied on an afternoon breeze sweeping over the coastal range to keep them cool.

Nonetheless, as she sat next to Jay, shoulder to shoulder, Kim had the sensation the summer sun was heating her. Warmth radiated from him as if his metabolism was turned up to high. She smiled, thinking that with a man like Jay, a woman wouldn't need an electric blanket on even the coldest arctic night. Her usually cold feet would not be a problem nor would she need a flannel nightgown. Hopefully no nightgown at all, she thought before she could stop herself.

"Hello, dears." Evie Anderson came swooping over in their direction, all gusto and enthusiasm, her potent perfume preceding her by several steps. "Aren't you the exclusive ones, sitting over here all by yourselves? I'm not sure you've had a chance to try my strawberry syrup. Made it from the plants in my own yard last year."

Jay groaned.

Her taste buds puckering, Kim pasted her professional smile on her face. "You know, Councilwoman Anderson, I'd really like to try your syrup, but I'm allergic to strawberries."

"Oh, that's too bad, child. How 'bout you, young man? Don't you know, Harlan raves about my syrup. The most unique he's ever tasted, he tells me. I'm sure he'd want you to try some."

"Please do," Kim urged him, practically biting her

cheek to keep from laughing. "I'm only sorry I can't enjoy the pleasure myself."

Jay coughed, choking, and Kim suspected behind his eye patches tears had formed.

"Yes, ma'am. Just a little. Maybe at the side of my plate."

"Of course, dear." The councilwoman poured a generous portion onto his plate. "Now you tell me if that isn't the best syrup you've ever tasted."

With an unsteady hand, he forked a bite of syrup-doused pancake into his mouth. A muscle flexed in his jaw before he swallowed, his Adam's apple bobbing two or three times.

"The chief's always right," he said tautly. "Unique."

"You're such a sweet boy." The councilwoman beamed her approval. "Would you like some more? There's plenty."

"No, no. Thanks anyway. I'm trying to watch my sugar intake."

Satisfied she'd made another conquest with her culinary skills, Evie Anderson wandered off to visit the innocents at the next table.

Kim stifled a laugh.

Turning, Jay leveled her a look that, despite his reflective glasses, was all too transparent. "You owe me, Ms. Lydell. Big time."

THEY'D FINISHED breakfast and Kim was making a desperate effort to excuse herself. She'd spotted more than one person sending a curious look in her direction. Being a TV personality, even on a small scale, in Paseo del Real, created a certain level of recognition. She didn't want anyone looking too closely.

"I've really got to go," she told Jay, edging away from their table.

"Sure, no problem." Standing, he looped his arm over her shoulder in a casual gesture. "There's this one thing I wanted to show you that we missed on the tour."

She got an uneasy feeling at the back of her neck. "I'm not going to slide down that pole of yours no matter what you think."

"Naw, I wouldn't make you do that."

Something about the cant of his lips suggested he had an idea even more troubling.

"Like what?" she asked.

"I've lost my bearings. Where's Engine 61?"

She glanced at the fire engines parked on the driveway in front of the station. "Out front. You want me to see something on the truck?"

"Yeah, something special. You'll like it, I promise."

Kim wasn't so sure, but she took his arm and helped him work his way through the unfamiliar maze of tables and chairs inside the station to the back of the fire truck.

"What am I supposed to see?" she asked.

"Ah, we've gotta climb up on top." He reached out, his hand searching for something to grip, and he hefted himself onto the gleaming step. "You need a hand?"

"I can manage." She pulled herself up. "Now what?"

"What do you say we go all the way?" Before she knew what was happening, he'd hooked his arm around her waist and was boosting her to the top of the fire truck where hoses were looped back and forth ready to be pulled free.

"Jay! What are you doing?"

He climbed up beside her. "Watch out for the couplings. They hurt like hell in the small of your back."

She barely glimpsed the shiny couplings that connected one section of fire hose to another before Jay had pressed her down on top of the canvas hoses.

"Now tell me, blue eyes. Did you see the movie *Backdraft?*"

She had, with all the sensual activity that took place on top of a fire truck. "No, Jay, you can't do this. There are people—"

"Yeah, right. But I can't see them...and they can't see us."

With unerring accuracy, his hand cupped her face and his mouth closed over hers.

Immediately she was caught up in the forbidden thrill of kissing a man when there were dozens of people around.

"Ever since that movie, I've wanted to do this," he whispered. "With you."

He deepened the kiss this time, and she opened to his penetration, welcoming it in ways she might have lacked the courage to accept when they were younger. She stirred against him, excited by the feel of his long, hard body pressed against hers. Beneath her the ranks of hose shifted, and she curled one leg around back of his, relishing the thrust of his arousal against the V of her thighs.

She'd had no idea as an adolescent how right Jay would feel in her arms. A perfect fit, both emotionally and physically.

She clung to him, her fingers threading their way through the short strands of hair on his head, wishing he'd left it long so she could more fully enjoy the weight and texture of the walnut-brown waves that had once curled at his nape.

There was a tenderness about him, taking her almost gently, and she wondered if he would have had as much control ten years ago. For her, after all these years, her passion rode higher, more experienced, more needy for what she wanted.

He tasted of strawberry syrup with a unique tang that was potently masculine, singularly Jay's own, a flavor she'd instinctively sought all of her life.

His hand covered her breast in a greedy embrace.

"I can't tell you how many years I've wanted to do that," he murmured against her lips.

"We shouldn't..." Her protest was mild even to her own ears. Spontaneously she tilted her hips toward his, and the desire she felt made her words a lie.

The alarm that could raise men from deep sleep sounded, the tone cutting through the air of the fire station. The dispatcher announced in the metallic sound of a loudspeaker where the emergency existed.

Jay cursed under his breath. ''We gotta get outta here.''

Together, they scrambled off the top of the fire engine, barely making it before the men on duty had taken their places on the fire engine and the truck had rolled out of the station.

Kim breathed deeply, trying to suppress the flow of desire that had nearly consumed her, and forcing herself to recall that she and Jay had nothing in common—except a mutual case of sexual attraction.

''Kimberly, is that you?'' Her mother's hard-edged voice that could slice through the most difficult scientific theory cut through Kim's lingering haze of passion. ''What on earth were you doing up on top of that fire truck?''

Chapter Six

Torn between mortification and laughter, Kim adjusted her scarf and tried to ignore the blush that burned her cheeks.

"Hello, Mother. I'm glad you could come."

Maureen DeMille-Lydell eyed Jay suspiciously. No taller than Kim, she wore her graying hair as she always had, a short wash-and-wear cut that required little attention beyond an occasional combing. Fashion was not an issue that concerned her.

"Yes, well, we do try to support our fire department. Your father was sorry he couldn't get away. There was a symposium today on particle physics that he and Leanne wanted to attend."

"I'm sure they'll find it fascinating." Symposiums had always held more allure for her father and sister than Kim's more prosaic interests. "Mother, I'd like you to meet Jay Tolliver. He was the firefighter who rescued me after the earthquake."

He extended his hand. "Glad to meet you, Mrs. Lydell."

She shook his hand warmly. "It's Doctor DeMille-

Lydell actually.'' Her title and hyphenated name were
a point of honor with Kim's mother, a remnant of her
days as an active women's libber. ''I'm pleased to
meet you. It was courageous of you to stay with her
when the building might have fallen down at any moment.''

''All part of the job, ma'am.'' He turned to Kim.
''Why don't you see that your mother gets some pancakes. I'll just go check on my Seeing Eye dog.''

He walked away, leaving Kim's mother slack-
jawed and momentarily speechless, and Kim holding
her breath as he nearly collided with a clutch of firefighters' wives chatting together. Fortunately one of
them snared Jay and redirected him toward where
Buttons was leashed.

''His Seeing Eye—'' Maureen frowned. ''Is he really blind?''

''He was in an explosion about ten days ago. He'd
given his helmet to one of the fire victims he was
rescuing….'' Just as he'd done for her in the earthquake, Kim recalled. ''Some glass blew up in his face
and cut the corneas in both his eyes. He's wearing
patches now.''

''How unfortunate for him. But really, Kimberly, I
don't mean to be disapproving, and I'm sure he's a
very brave man, but it was fairly obvious what you
were doing on top of the fire truck. And with a fireman at that. I know you're grateful for what he—''

''I wasn't kissing him out of gratitude, if that's
what you're thinking.'' Her mother would be even
more shocked to know Kim regretted the interruption

of an emergency, as foolish as that might seem. She could have gone on kissing Jay for hours.

"I was only thinking of your best interests, dear, and your image in the community. You're at a vulnerable point in your life and I know you're sensitive about your scars."

Kim bristled. "He can't see them, Mother."

"Yes, dear, that's the whole point. Simply because you've found a man who doesn't object to the dreadful damage that light fixture did to your face doesn't mean you have to take up with a fireman."

"*Firefighter,* that's the politically correct term now. Would you be happier if I took up with a blind Nobel Prize-winning scientist?"

"You're being obtuse, dear. I'd hate for you to make a mistake by doing anything hasty now when there's still a chance the new specialist will be able to repair the scars."

Her parents had lined up an appointment for her with yet another in a long line of plastic surgeons, this one in Santa Barbara. Kim supposed she should be grateful. Instead she resented the fact that her parents couldn't accept a daughter who was anything less than perfect. And that included her finding a *perfect* husband, one who met their high standards: intellectually gifted, a flawless physical specimen, someone who could sire impeccable grandchildren for her.

It had always struck Kim as odd that her mother would have such a woman's lib attitude about her own life yet have such traditional, albeit high expectations, for her younger daughter.

Jay wouldn't have met their standards as a high-school beau; they still wouldn't approve of Kim having a relationship with him.

What her mother didn't realize was that no relationship would be possible once Jay was able to see again.

Regaining his vision was something Kim sincerely hoped would happen soon, for Jay's sake. But the awful truth was, an evil, selfish part of Kim wanted to delay that moment, to hoard these few days—a week or two—when he couldn't see her. Wouldn't pity her. A time while she could store up memories to ease the bitter shock of that wrenching sensation when he was sure to turn his back on her.

A time when it didn't matter that they had nothing in common.

She clamped down on the threat of tears that had her chin trembling in anger at her mother...and maybe at fate itself.

"Would you like some pancakes, Mother?" she asked sweetly. "Councilwoman Anderson made some special strawberry syrup to go with them."

"No, dear, I really can't stay. I just wanted to show my support, and now I must be on my way. The afternoon speakers at the symposium looked quite interesting. I thought I'd drop by."

"Of course. Thanks for coming."

JAY HEADED for the far reaches of the fire station, a place where he could be alone. Not that being blind didn't isolate him more thoroughly than any amount of distance could.

And make him more stupid, too.

What the *hell* had he been thinking?

Another one of his jokes, getting Kim up on top of the fire truck with him. Payback time for Mrs. Anderson's god-awful strawberry syrup that tasted like she'd dumped in a bottle of lemon juice instead of sweetener.

In a savage swipe, he kicked the old picnic table the day-shift employees used for coffee breaks hard enough to send pains shooting up his shin bone. *Great!* If he handled things any better, he'd be off the job for months with a broken leg even if he did get his sight back. And it would damn well serve him right.

He had no business kissing Kim. No business wanting her sweet, hot body under his—on top of the fire truck or in his bed, he didn't care where. And he had no business embarrassing her in front of his friends— and her mom, for God's sake.

If he'd been thinking at all, it certainly hadn't been with any part of his anatomy above his waist.

He could lust all he wanted after Kimberly Lydell, just as he had in high school, but he still couldn't have her. Not now and maybe not even if he had a pair of fully functional eyes. He imagined that her Ph.D. mother had made that perfectly clear to her prom-queen daughter even if Kim had already recognized for herself they weren't exactly an ideal match.

God, when had he last read anything except *Sports Illustrated?* And the only sculpture he knew about was one of Father Junipero Serra, the founder of a string of missions in California. Jay had seen that one up close because a high-school buddy had thrown him into the fountain that surrounded the statue in downtown Paseo.

Sitting on the edge of the picnic table, he plowed his fingers through his hair. If Kim was so damn unsuited for him, why did the lingering taste of her lips taunt him so powerfully he wanted to go storming back into the fire station, find her and haul her off cave-man style, and not give a flying fig what her mother or anyone else thought?

He heard footsteps on the concrete pad and inhaled deeply, knowing he wouldn't have to look far to find Kim. She was wearing a tropical, sultry scent today, erotic and tantalizing. His body responded with a physical ache he had trouble suppressing.

"Is your mother already gone?" he asked as casually as he could.

Her footsteps halted. "How do you do that?"

His body tightened with heightened arousal at the lustrous sound of her voice—like a diamond amid chunks of coal. "Do what?"

"Know that I'm here when you can't see me."

"Emma Jean's psychic abilities are probably rubbing off on me."

"Yeah, right." She cocked her head, studying Jay, the way his forehead furrowed into two deep vertical grooves when he was troubled—or pouting. "Mother had more pressing matters to attend to, but you certainly escaped in a hurry."

"After she'd spotted us on top of the fire truck, I didn't think she'd be impressed by the bulge in my pants."

"I was," she admitted softly.

His pout shifted into a half smile. "Come on, blue eyes, face it. Your Ph.D. mother can't exactly be pleased about you hanging around with a firefighter. A blind one at that."

"I'm nearly thirty years old. I pretty much make up my own mind about who I see and who I don't."

His expression didn't change and all she could see was the distorted image of herself in the reflective lenses of his dark glasses. The noise of the visitors to the pancake breakfast was muted by the building that was between them and the crowd, leaving them apart from the others as effectively as their injuries isolated them from those who were whole.

"This isn't going to work, you know," he said quietly.

Her throat tightened just the same way it would if she was about to be dumped by an old boyfriend. "Just what is it that's not going to work?"

"You and me. If we act on this…sizzle that's between us, somebody's going to get hurt."

"We're adults." *What on earth was she saying?* She didn't want to have a physical relationship with Jay. *She'd* be the one who was hurt as soon as he got a good look at her face. In the long run, they had nothing in common.

"Sometimes that's the problem. We know exactly what we're missing."

She could only guess what it would be like with Jay. Slow and gentle, extraordinarily tender. Then hot, like the fires he fought, and fast moving. One glance at his hands that were curled around the edge of the table on either side of his lean hips, and she could easily imagine his caresses sparking a flame that could be quenched in only one way. And then only temporarily until he touched her again.

"Maybe you're right." Her pulse pounded in her chest and echoed much lower in her body with even a more frantic beat. "Maybe we shouldn't start something we couldn't stop."

She turned to leave and his hand reached out, capturing her wrist. "You're wearing sandals today and they make little slapping noises when you walk. And your perfume's a tropical scent, a little fruity, different than the floral one you were wearing the other day. That's how I knew you'd come looking for me. But even before, in high school, I knew where you were—all the time."

Staring at him dumbfounded, she tried to still her rocketing pulse even as his hand slid down to clasp his fingers with hers. "I didn't think you even noticed me."

"Every guy in school *noticed* you. I was obsessed."

"Why didn't you—"

"I was working two jobs and helping my mother at home. There wasn't much time left over for idle chitchat and I sure didn't have enough money to take you to the prom.''

"I would have settled for a soda or even a little conversation.''

"Would you?'' His brows lifted above the line of his dark glasses, pleating his forehead. "As I recall, I would have had to work my way through a pretty big crowd of guys to get within ten feet of you.''

She didn't dare admit that with one crook of his little finger, she would have come to him. But not now, not when this *sizzle* between them could so easily get out of hand.

"I've dated a lot of men, but never anyone special.'' No one but Jay had ever struck a chord in Kim that resonated so deeply, so mysteriously. Beyond the inherent danger he seemed to represent, she wasn't sure why she'd never quite forgotten the aloof young man who had so fascinated her. Perhaps she'd sensed a depth in Jay that was lacking in the other men she'd met—that drive that forced him to work two jobs to help his mother.

"You've never been engaged?'' he asked.

"Not even once.''

"Sounds like every man in the state must be even more blind than I am. Or fools.''

In spite of herself, his words sent a curl of pleasure through her midsection. "If it reassures you any, I have had a fair number of proposals. On average, when I'm on the air, I get two or three a week, some of them quite bizarre, like from inmates of the state correctional facility in Lompoc.''

His hand tightened convulsively around hers. "My God, you don't respond, do you?"

"No, those I pretty well ignore." And like most celebrities, even those in small towns, she had an unlisted phone number and a state-of-the-art security system at her home. "Guess one of the advantages of being off the air is that I haven't had a proposal in months."

"Don't even joke about that stuff, blue eyes." He nearly growled the warning. "Some of those men could be dangerous."

"I know." With her free hand, she cupped his cheek, cherishing his concern for her safety. "I watch my step and carry pepper spray. Fortunately, Paseo del Real isn't exactly a high-crime area."

"There are kooks everywhere."

Touched by his fear for her, she stood on tiptoe and brushed a quick kiss to his lips. She'd only meant it as an affectionate gesture, but the sizzle was instantaneous, igniting like a flash fire, that was just as quickly doused when two children came running and shouting into the secluded part of the fire station.

Gasping for breath, Kim jumped back as if she'd been shot, hiding her hands behind her back and instinctively ducking the scarred side of her face away from the new arrivals. This was certainly a day for her getting caught in one compromising position after another.

"Hey, Jay," a boy of about nine called as he dodged out of the grasp of his younger sister.

''Not fair,'' she complained. ''It's your turn to be it.''

''You gotta catch me first.'' Grinning, he whirled away again.

''Children! Enough already.'' An attractive dark-haired woman in her thirties appeared, mildly exasperated with having to chase after her offspring. She eyed Jay and Kim with open curiosity, and smiled. ''Hi, Jay, it's Janice Gainer. Sorry if we interrupted anything private.''

Kim couldn't remember a single day in her entire life when she'd blushed more frequently, with the small exception of the high-school dance when she dragged toilet paper around on the bottom of her shoe for hours before someone told her.

''No problem,'' Jay said. ''I was just showing Kim the station house.''

''Well, I'm sure this picnic table out here in back was the highlight of the tour.'' With a teasing laugh, she extended her hand to Kim. ''Hi, I'm Janice. My husband Ray is on C shift with Jay, except he's on the ladder truck. And these noisy creatures who interrupted your, ah, tour are Kevin and Maddie. We were just taking a shortcut out the back way to our car.''

In response to the introduction, the little girl wrapped her arms around her mother's hips and smiled shyly up at Kim with big, brown eyes.

''Glad to meet you.'' Kim included Maddie in her greeting.

"What happened to your face?" the little girl asked.

"Hush, Maddie. It's not polite—"

"It's all right." Kim quickly intervened, though it took all of her courage to hold her ground and not turn away. Or run away. "I was in an accident," she told the child.

Janice appeared horrified her daughter had brought attention to Kim's injuries. "I'm sorry...."

Kim waved off her apology. So much for her scarf as an effective cover for her scars.

Recognition dawned in Janice's eyes. "Say, aren't you the woman on TV—"

"Whom I heroically rescued after the earthquake," Jay inserted. "She's researching a story on me. All the brave deeds I've done."

"Uh-huh." Janice didn't look convinced. "Say, maybe you can bring Kim to the softball game tomorrow afternoon. You always get the most hits—" She gasped, color tingeing her cheeks. "Gosh, I'm sorry, Jay. Between my daughter and me, we certainly know how to put our feet in it today. I forgot you can't see. I guess that means you won't—"

"Won't play?" he interrupted. "Of course I will. Kim's going to be my coach."

Her head snapped around. "I am?"

"Sure. When I'm standing up at the plate you tell me when to swing." With an exaggerated frown, he puzzled over that proposition for a moment. "Or maybe you can be the hitter and I'll run for you. We'll see which works out best."

"You wouldn't get much exercise, I'm afraid, if I'm the one who has to hit the ball. Softball was never my forte, along with anything else remotely athletic. The ball usually hits me instead of the other way around."

"We'll work something out," Jay assured them, then turned to Janice. "Say, where was Ray this morning? Didn't he come to the breakfast?"

Looking uncomfortable, Janice didn't immediately respond, instead she glanced away. "He had something else he needed to do this morning. You know how there's never enough time to get everything done with the crazy hours you firefighters work."

Jay seemed to accept that answer, but Kim suspected there was more going on between Janice and her husband than simply a lack of time to get his chores done.

"Mom, are you coming?" Kevin shouted, apparently losing interest in the metal gate he'd been using as a swing. "I've got Little League."

"I'm coming, dear." Janice waved to her impatient son, then said to Kim, "I hope you'll come to the game. We have a picnic, too, sort of a potluck. Everything starts about noon. We wives have a good time visiting while the guys pretend they're still nineteen years old. Then we take 'em home and give 'em rubdowns for all their aching muscles."

"Hey, I like the sound of that," Jay said with a wicked grin. "Why don't we just skip the game part and get right on with the rubdown? Whaddaya say, Kim? We can take turns."

Janice laughed, and Kim felt like blushing again. The man was determined to permanently stain her cheeks red.

Gathering her children, Janice said goodbye and hustled the youngsters out the back gate normally used by the paramedic truck.

Jay waited until their footsteps faded. He'd been shaken by the idea of hundreds of guys proposing to Kim, kooks or not. And then her quick kiss had rocked him back on his heels again.

He folded his hands into fists. *He didn't want anyone kissing her except him!* He didn't want them even *thinking* about it. But what the hell position was he in to stop every Tom, Dick and Harry from doing what they damn well pleased? Blind as a bat, he wouldn't even be able to protect Kim from a crazed stalker if he walked right up and snatched her away. Some kind of a hero he made!

She cleared her throat. "I think I'd better be going too."

Raw panic gripped him. She'd walk away and who knew what kind of man would hit on her—*propose* to her, for God's sake. It didn't matter that she thought she was ugly. Jay didn't believe it, not in a million years, and no man in his right mind would either. Her scars, no matter how bad, were only skin deep. On the inside Kimberly Lydell was beautiful. Unfair to Kim or not, he desperately wanted to build a wall around her and keep her all to himself.

"I'm going to need a really good coach," he said

nonchalantly, "if I'm going to avoid getting beaned at the game tomorrow."

"You could *not* play. That way you wouldn't get hit." Her suggestion was all too helpful.

"No, that's not an option. See, I have this reputation to maintain. Sort of the Sammy Sosa of C shift. I mean, guys bet money on me. I wouldn't want to fail them this year just because of a little problem with my eyes."

"A little problem."

"Right. But with you coaching—"

"If I didn't think you were crazy enough to get up there on your own, I wouldn't even consider participating in this charade."

He grinned and wanted to push his fist in the air as a sign of victory. She'd fallen for his gambit. "You're all heart."

"What I am is resourceful. The Braille Institute has baseballs that make a noise so their blind clients— mostly kids, allow me to point out—can hear them coming and they don't get their skulls cracked open. Not that your hard head would be seriously affected, but I'll see if I can borrow a couple of those for the game tomorrow."

He frowned. "I don't want to have any advantage over the other guys." He wanted her to think of him as *normal,* not handicapped.

"Fine by me. All you have to do is convince everyone on the field to play the game blindfolded. I'll pick you up about eleven-thirty."

He sensed her turning away, then heard the soft

slap-slap of her sandals on the concrete as she departed. A moment later, only her scent lingered—and the curse he'd left hanging in the air.

He'd never wanted a woman more—a woman he'd never be allowed to have. Even when he got his sight back—and damn it, he would!—she'd still be out of his class.

Hell, he'd never even met a Ph.D. until he'd met Kim's mother. Kim's family was full of 'em and probably none of them knew the difference between a clamp and a piton.

And a beautiful woman like Kim? Shoot, whatever scarring she was worried about wouldn't count with any man worth his salt. She'd have her choice of men who were a helluva lot smarter and richer than Jay ever expected to be. Men who'd read a decent book recently.

MOST OF THE PANCAKE breakfast crowd had left, and Jay made his way upstairs in the station house to the oversize locker in his room, digging out his workout shorts, shirt and running shoes. From the smell, he suspected he hadn't washed them since his last shift— the day of his accident.

He decided to worry about that later and changed clothes. There was a lot of pent-up energy in him that needed to be worked off. Frustration. Anger—at himself and the tiny shards of glass that had impaled themselves in his corneas.

The primal need that was driving him to do stupid things when it came to Kim.

And the irritating fact she didn't seem to give a damn.

Hell! A musical softball. What was she thinking? That he was a sap who needed pity, no doubt. Someone who was less than a man.

The workout room was in the basement in what used to be a boiler room. He heard someone on the stair-stepper moving at a quick pace, but he didn't acknowledge their presence. One thing about being blind, it was easy to pretend you were alone.

He climbed on the treadmill, set the speed and angle at something he hoped wouldn't kill him, and started running. But he guessed he could run all the way to Timbuktu and still not feel he was good enough for Kim. He wondered if his mother had inadvertently taught him that, or if it had been the bureaucrats who periodically had threatened to remove him to a foster home. Either way, he'd been trying to prove himself for about as long as he could remember.

Proving himself to an absent father.

The thought came out of nowhere. As if some man whose face Jay had never known would be all that important to him. A man he'd spent a great deal of time loathing because he'd deserted him and his mom. Had left *Jay* the head of the family.

Sweat dripped down his temples and he increased the speed, pounding along on the treadmill as if he could outrun his blindness. The poverty in which he'd been raised. Some deep-seated inadequacy he'd felt all of his life. Only here, in the brotherhood of the fire service, had he felt whole. And a rotten accident had taken that brotherhood from him.

But brought Kim back to him, he realized with a start that made him lose his balance.

Staggering, half falling off the machine, he grabbed frantically for the controls and shut off the damn treadmill. Breathing hard, he tried to slow the pounding in his chest.

"Good-lookin' woman you were with today," the man on the stair-stepper commented, hardly breathing hard at all given the pace he was going.

"Diaz, that you?"

"Yep." The stairs kept clicking along without missing a beat. Diaz, on A shift, was not a large man, but he made up for his height and weight by dint of sheer muscle power and determination.

"How many hours do you do that stuff?" Jay asked peevishly.

"As many as it takes."

Leaning over, Jay folded his arms across the treadmill console and rested his head on his arms. "She's the most beautiful woman I've ever known," he said so softly he wasn't sure Diaz would hear him.

"She's a lucky lady to have caught your interest, *compadre.* Very lucky."

Jay wanted to believe that but it wasn't easy. Not after so many years of feeling inadequate. Not when he was blind.

KIM DROVE UP the canyon road, paused to get her mail at the roadside box, and turned her car into the

tree-shaded driveway to her house. Her sudden arrival
startled a white-tailed deer who'd been grazing on a
patch of new spring grass. The doe dashed for the
cover of mesquite shrubs and California live oaks,
probably in the hope of drawing Kim away from her
fawn who was lying so still in the shadows he was
almost impossible to spot.

When Kim had bought the house, the isolation and
rural atmosphere had appealed to her need for quiet
and space, with the added bonus that she'd still be
only twenty minutes from the TV studio. She had
plenty of excitement on the job, and with her public
appearances to promote the station, as much social
interaction as she cared to handle. Here, in the soli-
tude of her own home, she could recharge her batter-
ies, indulge in her solitary hobbies. Unlike most of
her canyon neighbors, she'd even planted bushes and
ground cover that would attract deer to browse, and
she cherished their regular visits.

She parked the car at the side of the house and got
out. Only the buzz of a flying insect and the ticking
of her car as it cooled broke the gentle blanket of
silence.

Inside the house the quiet was just as deep.

The potted plants she religiously fed and watered,
their leaves glistening in a dozen different shades and
textures of green, silently greeted her. She automatically plucked a couple of dying blossoms from a
thriving African violet plant and checked the moisture
of the soil. In a sunny part of her yard she had a small
greenhouse where she grew a few orchids and forced

hyacinths into early blooms for a splash of winter color.

Dropping the mail on an end table next to an exquisite sculpture of a wild mustang, she stood in the middle of the living room, her purse still slung over her shoulder, gazing out at the landscape through a wide plate-glass window. Rolling, tree-studded hills gave way to a fertile valley at the bottom of the canyon where farmers labored over string beans and artichokes. In the distance, the Pacific Ocean lay hidden in a bright haze.

Suddenly, she shivered and wished Jay's big orange cat were here to curl up with on the couch.

Better yet, she wished she could curl up with Jay.

Since the earthquake, her home had been her refuge, the isolation a balm to soothe her shattered dreams as well as her facial injuries. Somehow she'd turned the seclusion of these five acres into a prison of her own making.

She tugged the scarf from her head and let it trail from her fingers as she walked down the hallway into her bedroom.

Being seen in public had not caused the earth to shift on its axis. No one except a small child had even commented on Kim's scars—out of politeness, no doubt, because she had caught more than one curious look. But unlike a vampire who risked death away from his crypt, Kim had survived her sojourn in sunlight.

Perhaps it was time she rejoined the human race.

Slipping out of her silk blouse, she hung it in the

closet, oddly aware that no men's clothing had ever hung beside hers, shoulder to shoulder, waistband to waistband, her perfume mixing with the muskier scent of a male. She pictured Jay's sharply pressed uniforms lined up in a row next to her pastel-colored suits and smiled.

A picnic she could handle, she decided, but no way was she going to let some lunatic firefighter force her to play baseball—blindfolded or any other way.

She finished changing into jeans and a lightweight sweater, then went back into the living room to open the mail—a handful of ads, an electric bill and a letter from KPRX. She opened that one first.

The initial paragraph took two tries before the impact of all the legalese sank in—*pursuant to the personal services contract between the party of the first part—Kimberly Lydell—and the contracting organization—KPRX-TV, a California Corporation—the leave of absence of the party of the first part has been terminated, effective this date.*

Kim sat down heavily on the arm of the couch to finish the rest of the letter. They'd *fired* her. Not one word from her boss or the station owner. No opportunity for another chance or to apply for an off-air job. Just an impersonal letter announcing there'd be no more paychecks coming. And furthermore, given her general good health, they would appeal any adverse rulings regarding disability payments—she wasn't, after all, an employee but a contract person. Ineligible for workmen's compensation. Reimbursement for medical expenses would be considered on a case-by-case basis.

Anger and fear churned a bitter soup in her stomach.

Dammit, they owed her more than a brush-off! Sure the broadcasting business was fickle. But it was *their* building that had collapsed. *She* hadn't done anything wrong.

Crushing the letter in her fist, she marched into the spare room she used as her home office, snatched up the phone and dialed the TV station. It took three rings before Harriet Bigelow answered with a cheery, "KPRX-TV, your independent television station serving the central coast since 1972. How may I help you?"

"Harriet, this is Kim. I'd like to speak to Mr. Woodward."

The pause on the other end of the line seemed inordinately long. "I'm sorry Kim, he's not here today. He rarely is on Saturday."

That took some of the steam out of her fury, at least for the moment. "Of course. I forgot. I'll catch him at home then."

"Oh, he won't be there," Harriet offered brightly. "He left for New York yesterday."

The day Kim's letter had been postmarked. "New York? What's happening there?"

"Well, don't say I said so, but there's a rumor going around that we may become a network affiliate. Wouldn't that be great?"

Harriet's cheerfulness cut right through to Kim's

despair. There'd be no chance now to work her way up through the ranks of network anchorwomen to bigger TV markets where she'd be able to cover national news stories. No chance at all now that she'd been fired.

Her throat filled with the acid tears of disappointment. All along she had hoped—

''When do you expect him back?''

''Oh, not till the end of the week. Lots of wining and dining to do back there with the big boys, huh?''

Kim tried to thank Harriet, but she couldn't get out a single sound.

As she silently cradled the phone, she realized she'd not only lost her chance at a network job, but the absence of a paycheck meant her mortgage payments would soon be at risk.

Closing her eyes, she mentally calculated the bottom line of her savings account. A few months without a job and she'd fall into arrears on her payments.

A few months after that she'd either be homeless or dependent upon her parents.

The mere thought of either possibility had her stomach churning again.

Chapter Seven

Jay waved in Kim's general direction from home plate. "Come on, Kim. We're up."

"What *we?*" she complained. "I told you I couldn't hit a basketball with a baseball bat, even on a good day."

"Well, I certainly can't do it alone." With exaggerated effort, he took a swing at the air and stumbled across the plate, finally righting himself on the opposite side. "You don't want C shift to lose because of you, do you?"

Janice Gainer, with whom she'd been sitting at the picnic table, laughed. "Now he's put the outcome of the game on your shoulders, I think you're going to have to give in."

"Right," she groaned. The entire firefighter brotherhood—wives and children included—appeared to be on Jay's side. After a sleepless night worrying about her own future, it was a relief not to have to consider anything more important than a softball rivalry among friends.

She'd picked Jay up this morning and driven him

to the regional park for the picnic and annual challenge game between A and C shifts. His buddies had welcomed him with open arms while she'd slipped over to a picnic table already covered with a variety of dishes and added her bowl of spicy red bean salad she'd hastily put together. Immediately the wives had made her feel at home.

Despite their curious stares and unspoken questions—both about her scars and her relationship with Jay—she'd been having a good time taking a back seat, listening to them talk about their husbands and children.

Had they been discussing Russia's problems with its provinces or the wildly fluctuating stock market, Kim would have been able to contribute to the conversation, but expertise about husbands and children had eluded her. The giant hole in her experience was all too obvious among this group of women. And at her core, a twinge of regret reminded Kim she might have missed something important.

Janice gave her a little nudge with her elbow. "Go forth, have fun. And remember to keep your eye on the ball and get out of the way."

The players on the field all cheered when she stood up.

With a troubled shake of her head, Kim walked toward home plate and Jay. "Why do I have the feeling we're both about to get beaned?"

He grinned and held out the bat to her. "You haven't got a thing in the world to worry about. Ol' Sampson out there on the mound can't pitch faster than, say, fifty or sixty miles an hour. Won't hardly hurt at all.''

She rolled her eyes. ''That's not very reassuring.''

The bat was heavy and awkward in her hands. She'd once tried out for the high-school drill team, but lacking even minimal coordination, had never participated in sports. The drama club had been her thing. ''Jay, I don't even know how to swing a bat. There's no way I'm going to hit anything.''

''I'll show you.''

He gathered her back against him, his arms around her, his hands closing around hers on the bat, her spine curved against his chest and stomach. If they hadn't been in a public park with dozens of onlookers, the pose could have become intimate. Now it seemed, well, familiar. And a promise of what might be.

''Hmm, you're wearing jeans today,'' he whispered softly, his breath warm on her ear. ''I like you in denim. And you've got on that flowery perfume again.''

A ripple of awareness shuddered through her. For a blind man, he was certainly observant.

The men on the playing field waited patiently for Jay to finish teaching Kim the rudiments of batting. Virtually all of them were smiling in a knowing way that made Kim feel self-conscious both about her scars and what they must think of her relationship with Jay. Coming with him today might have been a very bad mistake after all. At this point in her life— ugly as sin and unemployed—she had little to offer any man.

Even less to a man who was a natural athlete.

"Okay," Jay explained. "When Sampson pitches, we're going to swing the bat like this." He demonstrated. "All we have to do is keep our swing level and we'll get a hit. I promise."

"I'm really sorry I didn't get that ball from the Braille Institute so you could do this on your own." The letter from KPRX had so shaken her, she'd forgotten her promise to get that special ball until it was too late and the Institute was closed for the weekend.

"Not to worry. The other guys wouldn't agree to playing blindfolded anyway." He took another practice swing with her. "Perfect. A home run."

Kim didn't think so. "Wouldn't we do better if we were standing somewhere near home plate?"

"We're not?"

"About three feet off the mark, I'd say."

"Well, shoot, blue eyes. It's your job to start us off in the right place."

Kim could only imagine what a ridiculous sight they made, the two of them standing up at the plate like Siamese twins, her butt linked to his pelvis. The catcher crouched behind them; the infielders moved up close and the outfielders jogged in so they were practically standing on the base path. But Jay's teammates cheered them on from the dugout and the families had gathered around to watch the spectacle.

Definitely a Kodak moment, she realized and she grinned in spite of herself.

"Ready?" Sampson asked.

"No," Kim insisted.

"Anytime you are," Jay contradicted.

The ball leaped out of the pitcher's hand. Instinctively Kim closed her eyes.

"Strike one!"

"No way!" Jay complained to the umpire. "The ball was a mile outside the plate. Are you blind, or something?"

The spectators whooped and hollered.

Jay tugged her close again and took another practice swing with the bat. "We'll get 'em this time, sweetheart. Keep your eye on the ball."

"So I can watch it hit me in the head?"

"No, so you can tell me when to duck."

This time she kept her eyes open. She had the feeling the pitcher was throwing the ball as slowly as he could and still get it to the plate, but she managed to get her swing going milliseconds after the catcher already had the ball in his glove.

"Strike two!"

"See, we're getting better already," Jay said. "This time it'll be out of the park."

Actually, Kim was looking forward to strike three so she could go sit down again among the onlookers.

Looking like he was going to fire the next ball right down the pike, Sampson wound up and lobbed one toward the plate. Kim gritted her teeth and swung with all her might. Magically, the ball hit the bat and dribbled a few feet out in front of the plate.

"We hit it!" The feeble effort was laughable but at least they'd connected with the ball. Kim couldn't help but feel a surge of pride.

"Then we've gotta run." Jay took her by the hand, half dragging her toward first base, the bat still in her free hand.

Meanwhile, the fans were cheering and the opposing players were clowning around trying to delay the throw to first base by dropping the ball and scooping it up again before tossing it at the very last moment to throw them out.

By the time Kim stumbled across the bag, she was laughing so hard she could barely stand up and was at serious risk of wetting her pants.

She was also called "Out!" by the umpire.

"That's it," she said, gasping for breath. "My baseball career is over as of this moment."

Casually, Jay looped his arm over her shoulders, not breathing hard at all. "You can't desert me now."

"Oh, yes I can." Scooting out from under his arm, she turned him and pointed him toward the dugout, giving him a little push in that direction. "Next time one of your buddies can pinch-hit for you."

Still laughing, she escaped the baseball diamond and received a heroine's welcome from the firefighters' wives and their children. Despite a certain amount of embarrassment about Jay's shenanigans, she couldn't remember having more fun.

Even so, she didn't imagine she'd be applying for a job as a sportscaster anytime soon.

As THE GAME progressed, the wives lost interest and all except the youngest children wandered off to the nearby playground to enjoy the slides and swings.

Growing more at ease with the firefighters' wives, and always fascinated by people and how they lived, and accustomed to interviewing guests on TV, Kim began asking questions of the women sitting around her at the picnic table.

"I admit to an insatiable curiosity about people," she began, sipping on a can of cold pop someone had provided when she'd come back breathless from her foray into the sports world. She was keeping one eye on the baseball diamond, where Jay was playing right field with a buddy nearby, who she presumed could see better than he could. "When you send your husband off to work in the morning, does it bother you knowing he might have to risk his life to save someone else?"

"I try not to think about it," a woman sitting opposite her admitted. She had a baby in her lap who was less than six months old and an older boy who'd gone off to play with the other children. Little wonder she didn't want to consider losing her husband in a fire.

"At least when he's at work I know he's not out with some other woman," a second woman joked, a twinkle in her eyes. "And when he gets home, he's always glad to see me, if you know what I mean. Some mornings after his shift, I can hardly get the kids off to school fast enough."

The women laughed.

"Is that how come you've got four kids?" one asked.

"And they all attend summer school!"

The woman looked smug and not at all embarrassed by the remarks.

Another woman with a pixie-like face and glasses said, "When I imagine Stony at work, I think of him polishing the engine or doing physical training, not anything dangerous. Since he was a Marine when we got married and they kept deploying him to one hot spot after another where I knew he could get shot at, I'm happier with him as a firefighter. At least he's home more often."

"Bet you still have to drag out the garbage can every week," the woman with the baby added. "I swear they schedule these guys to miss garbage night on purpose."

That brought another round of laughter.

When they all quieted, Janice said, "It took me a long time to get used to the idea Ray could be hurt, or worse. I'm not sure I'm used to it yet. And every time I hear a siren..." She shrugged. "I guess it just comes with the territory."

The women settled into a pensive mood and Kim posed another question, she hoped on a less sensitive subject. "What about disciplining the children and handling household emergencies? With your husbands gone such long hours, how do you manage?"

"I discipline my kids whenever they need it— which isn't often," the woman at the end of the table hastened to add.

"If I can't fix something myself," Janice said, "I make a list for Ray of things that need to be done. Not that he actually *does* them, you understand."

Laughing, the other women at the table nodded their understanding. "But it makes me feel better. But say—" She gave Kim a curious look. "Are you thinking about joining the club?"

The implication was obvious: was Kim considering marrying Jay? She ducked her head away, realizing Janice and her friends had no idea how impossible that would be once Jay could see again.

"No," she whispered, her throat strangely achy. "That's not in the cards." Not now, not ever. Nor was she sure how she'd feel about being married to a man whose job put his life at risk, no matter how these other women had adjusted to the possibility. Perhaps she'd covered too many stories of dangerous fires with multiple victims, including firefighters.

A shout went up from the baseball diamond and everyone glanced in that direction.

To Kim's horror, Jay was sprawled face down on the dusty path between first and second base. Without thinking, she was on her feet and running as fast as she could toward him. The man was so *damned* determined to pretend he could do everything he could do before the accident, before he lost his sight—however temporarily. Swear to God, in the process, he was going kill himself!

She hadn't quite reached him when he'd begun struggling to his feet, shrugging off the helping hands of his buddies.

"I'm okay. I fell. No big deal."

Someone brushed the dust off the front of his shirt. He slapped the hand away. "Leave me alone!"

Slipping up beside him, Kim slid her arm through his. ''I don't know about you, Sammy Sosa, but I'm starving. You think we could get these people to serve lunch pretty soon?''

He tensed, like a bow that had been pulled too taut, and then relaxed. ''Good plan. C shift doesn't like to beat the opposition too badly, do we, guys?''

''Lunch sounds great,'' someone agreed.

Wordlessly, Logan handed Jay's dark glasses to Kim as she walked him off the field. She nodded her thanks, but her vision was almost as impaired at Jay's. Tears could do that to a woman.

So could a man with a mountain full of pride.

''NOTHING WRONG with your appetite,'' Kim commented as Jay finished off a heaping plateful of potato salad, beans, gelatin and two hot dogs smothered in mustard and pickle relish.

Jay had brought a blanket from home and they'd spread it out in a shady spot beneath a huge oak tree away from the crowd. He'd washed up after his spill on the softball field but there were still streaks of dirt on his face and his gray athletic shirt. His jeans were old, worn nearly white, with the beginning of a hole in one knee. Overall, he looked like a jock who'd had a rather bad day.

''The hard part is taking a bite of something, figuring you've got potato salad on your fork and discovering you've speared a sardine instead.''

''Life is full of little surprises.'' Like meeting the boy you had a crush on in high school, finding you like him even more as an adult—and then knowing you still had no future with him.

He set his plate aside and leaned back against the tree, his long legs stretched out in front of him. Against her will, her gaze lingered on the frayed zipper of his jeans and she wondered if his appetite for activities other than eating was equally robust. If his kiss of yesterday was any indication, bottomless would only begin to describe his reservoir of passion. Her skin flushed at the thought, an ache of need forming between her thighs.

She shifted uncomfortably.

Lifting his glasses, Jay rubbed at his eye patches.

"Did you get enough to eat?" he asked.

"More than enough. The ladies are good cooks."

"Half of that food, the guys made. One of the varied talents we firefighters pick up." He knuckled his right eye again.

Kim frowned. "I don't think you should be doing that."

"What? Cooking?"

"No, rubbing your eyes."

He shrugged. "Besides being a stickler for balanced meals, Logan's probably the best cook on our shift. He does a clam linguini that's great, and he's the one who usually cooks our holiday turkey and stuffs it with pecans and apples. He probably brought the pasta salad today. He'd make some woman a great wife."

She glanced over to the tables where Logan was eating with several of the firefighters who evidently didn't have families. When she glanced back, Jay was rubbing his eyes again. "What's your specialty?"

"Noodles and nothing."

"Sounds a little, uh, bland. What is it?"

"Oh, you usually put a little chicken and some veggies in it, but by the time the last guy gets any, all that's left is noodles and nothing. But it still tastes pretty good." He shook his head as if he were trying to dislodge something.

"What's wrong, Jay?"

"I don't know. It's like I've got burning rocks in both my eyes." Cursing, he pressed the heels of his hands into his eyes.

"Wait right here." Trying to keep her panic at bay, she hurriedly got to her feet and ran to the table filled with firefighters. "Are any of you paramedics?"

One man raised his hand. "What's wrong?"

"I think Jay's in trouble. His eyes are burning."

She never imagined a group of men could move so swiftly and with such calm efficiency. Within ten minutes they had Jay in the emergency room at Paseo del Real Community Hospital, and she was in the waiting room, desperately afraid he'd further damaged his eyes by taking a header in the dirt.

TENTACLES of fear clawed through Jay's chest. Like crawling into a structure fire, blackness enveloped him, smoke so thick he couldn't breathe through his mouthpiece, his air cut off. Drowning in darkness, he'd lost his way.

Red-hot embers tortured his eyes. Burning daggers lanced his corneas without bringing light.

He was blind. Totally blind.

He swore at his own stupidity. His pride.

"I'm here, Jay."

He focused on Kim's voice, husky with concern, lifting the veil of blackness around him. Instinctively he reached out to her and she took his hand, her fingers slender, almost fragile. He tried not to squeeze too tight but he desperately needed a lifeline. Something—someone—to draw him back from the fiery abyss of lifelong terror. *Dependency.*

She grazed her cheek along the back of his hand, her skin as smooth and soft as a peach. "You're going to be all right."

"The doctor—"

"Dr. Plum washed out your eyes with a special solution. You'd gotten dirt under the patches and he had to get that out. Now he's called a specialist. She should be here soon."

"When the doc took off my patches—" His throat worked convulsively but he couldn't seem to swallow his fear. "I couldn't see, Kim. A white light and a blur. Even without the patches that's all—"

"Shh, you'll be fine. We'll just wait for the specialist. I'll stay right here with you."

He'd been in the emergency room often enough on the job to be used to the murmured comings and goings of the hospital staff, the whispered concerns of patients and their families, and the antiseptic smell. Kim's faintly floral scent seemed out of place, something beautiful in a world that could be very ugly. A world where lives were turned upside down.

What if he'd never be able to see her again—not on a TV screen, not even from a distance? The genuine smile that lit up her whole face and made her eyes squint when she found something funny. The way her hair curled beside her jaw, inviting a kiss right at the juncture of her throat.

For years he'd limited himself to admiring her from afar. In high school he hadn't had much of a choice, given his other obligations. And when she'd returned to Paseo del Real she'd come back as a TV star, hardly in his class, and so he'd simply contented himself with watching her on the screen. Now he had no choice at all.

"Your friends are waiting in the lobby," she said. "Rather than overwhelming the emergency room with a dozen firefighters or so, they sent me in instead."

"Smart men. Florence Nightingale beats the heck out of an ugly fire jock any day."

"They're an amazing group of men—the wives, too. You're all really a family, aren't you?"

"Yeah. And I guess I blew the heck out of the family picnic, didn't I?" All because he'd been trying to prove to Kim and everyone else that he wasn't handicapped, that he could do anything any other man could do. *Including act like a fool.*

"I didn't hear any of them complaining."

"Only because they'd already had their lunch. You ought to hear the griping that goes on at the station when the tone goes off in the middle of dinner and we get a fire run. It's even worse if it's a false alarm. We've got this one lady, Abigail Trumblebird, who gets lonely about once a week and starts a fire in her wastebasket or something.''

Kim knew he was babbling out of anxiety and soothed her free hand across his forehead. Truth be told, she wanted to touch him in any way she could, concerned by the pinched way his dark brows were pulled together even while he was trying to act light-hearted.

''Are you in any pain? Is there something I can get for you while we're waiting?''

''I'm fine. Just ducky.''

She hated the way he got so flippant about his injuries, put up such a damn brave front, when she knew he must be scared to death. At least an ordinary mortal would be frightened. Jay wanted to be immune to the weaknesses of the flesh. But she didn't buy the act. He was too smart a man not to know his vision was in jeopardy from this new assault on his eyes. If only he hadn't been so determined to—

The curtain on the cubicle swept back with a whoosh of fabric. ''Mr. Tolliver?''

''That's me.''

''Dr. Muramic here. I'm going to have you moved to a different examination room where I can control the light. Your wife can come with you.''

The doctor, an angular woman close to six feet tall, swept out of the room with as much energy as she had entered. There wasn't time to correct her assumption about Kim's relationship to Jay. Nor did Kim particularly want to.

She planned to stick right with him through whatever examination Dr. Muramic had in mind.

Jay had once saved her life. And Kim knew, although Jay would be the last person to admit it, that he didn't want to be alone now. Because in the unusual pallor of his skin, she recognized his fear—just as he'd seen hers four months ago.

WITH BRUSQUE professionalism, Dr. Muramic made quick work of the examination, applied drops to Jay's eyes and covered his eyes with sterile bandages instead of the patches. She shoved her chair back from her patient and addressed Kim.

"I'm going to prescribe eye drops every three hours around the clock for three days. Given the initial injury to his corneas and now a further assault on his eyes, I'm very concerned about the possibility of infection."

"Are the corneas healing?" Jay asked.

"It's extremely difficult to tell, Mr. Tolliver, given the current inflammation. It would have been wiser to keep your head out of the dirt."

His hand flexed around Kim's. "Now why didn't I think of that?" he muttered.

"From now on I want you to take it easy. No vigorous exercise, lots of rest." The doctor turned to Kim. "Are you squeamish about giving eye drops, Mrs. Tolliver?"

"Not in the least."

"I can do it on my own."

"Nonsense. You can't see to fill the eye dropper."
The doctor scribbled out a prescription and handed it
to Kim. "You can take this to the pharmacy in the
lobby, they'll fill it for you. And have Mr. Tolliver
see his regular ophthalmologist at the end of the
week." With that, she marched out of the examining
room.

"What's the matter with that woman? She was
treating me like a damn kid. I can take care of myself."

"Not this time, buster."

"What are you going to do? Drive down to my
place every three hours just to give me some stupid
eye drops? That's ridiculous."

"You're absolutely right. Which is why, unless
you can think of somebody you'd rather have hanging
around, I'm going to be your roommate for the next
three days." *And nights,* she thought, with an un-
nerving spark of awareness.

Chapter Eight

Nighttime was the hardest. The dreams. Fighting off his fears.

As a kid, Jay had always had a night light. It kept the encroaching darkness at bay, tamed the shadowy monsters the street lights cast through his bedroom window, silenced the moan of the wind and creaking floor boards.

Now, as he lay in bed staring sightlessly at the ceiling, there was only blackness and a fear that had nothing to do with his imagination. Blindness—*permanent* blindness was a real possibility.

Kim had brought him home from the hospital, then gone to her place to pack a bag. She'd returned with Chinese takeout, which they'd eaten while watching "Sixty Minutes" on a big TV screen that might as well have been a giant boom box for all it mattered to him.

Across the hall he could hear her shifting restlessly on the narrow bed in the spare bedroom, the mattress so old it sagged in the middle, the springs squeaking. She'd be more comfortable here, with him. And he had no right to ask her. No right to want the scent of her on his sheets, her head pillowed next to his. Their two bodies sated yet still joined together.

In the distance, he heard the sparse traffic on Paseo Boulevard and the bleat of Engine 61's horn as it rolled out of the station house. He pictured Paulson, the driver on C shift, hitting the siren and the engine racing north in response to a call for help. Jay listened intently, trying to gauge the distance until he could no longer hear the siren wailing.

"Are you awake?"

She was standing at his bedroom door. He imagined her backlit by the hallway light, her body silhouetted through a sheer gown—the curve of her hips, her narrow waist, the swell of her breasts outlined in seductive detail.

"Yeah, I'm awake." And aroused, the blanket tenting over the evidence of his body's reaction to that which only his mind's eye could see.

"Time for more drops."

"You aren't going to get much sleep if you have to keep waking up every three hours." Neither was he, waiting for her. Wanting her.

"I suppose, given enough time, we could train Cat to do this. But by then, you won't need them any more." The bed tilted as she sat down on the edge. "Hang your head over the side for me."

He adjusted his position. "I really think I could handle drops myself."

"But then I'd miss all the fun, wouldn't I?"

She lifted the dressing from his right eye. There

was light, blurry as if he were inside a cloud, and all he could see was her shadowed shape. He swallowed convulsively as fear rose in his throat. With a force of will, he concentrated on her clean, fresh scent. Like springtime. If he never saw flowers again, never caught her fragrance again, he'd always remember this moment.

When she finished attending to both eyes, he shifted his head back to his pillow. "I guess I'm not a very good patient."

Her hand was cool on his forehead, stroking his hair. "You're fine. Try to get some sleep now."

He desperately didn't want her to leave, didn't want to be alone in the dark. "There's a reason why I'm such a lousy patient."

"Because you're a man?" There was a smile in her voice.

"No. Because of my mother." She met his words with quiet patience, not prodding but simply waiting for him to continue. "Among her assorted disabilities, she was a diabetic. She was scared to death she'd end up blind. The irony is, with all her troubles, she never lost her sight. I'm the one who's blind."

"Temporarily."

In the stillness of the night, in the quiet intimacy of his bedroom, it seemed easier to confess his fears than it was in the daylight, even if he couldn't see the difference. And in the darkness it was also impossible to pretend, to hide those fears any longer.

To disguise his terror that his blindness could be *permanent*.

"I'm scared, Kim. More afraid than I've ever been in a fire worrying about a roof collapsing or a flashover. I'm scared I won't ever be able to find my way out of this one."

"Of course you're afraid. Who wouldn't be? But you have to *believe*, Jay. Believe that you'll get your vision back, that you'll be fine. You aren't the kind of man who gives up." She rested her palm on his chest. "You're a man with heart."

He covered her hand with his, her fingers slender, her skin soft.

Something in the smoky quality of her voice persuaded him to trust her, to *believe*. He knew that was part of her success as a news anchorwoman. The viewers never doubted what she said was true. She *knew*. And everyone who heard her believed exactly what she told them.

"God, you should have been a preacher."

She chuckled, low and husky, a little startled by his remark. "Why would you say a thing like that?"

"Because if you told me I could walk on water, I'd damn well try."

"You can, Jay Tolliver. As far as I'm concerned, you've always been able to do anything you wanted to."

"And you still won't go scuba diving with me?"

"Walking *on* water is a whole lot different than thrashing around *under* it. I'll leave that pleasure to you."

He felt the gentle touch of her lips on his, a sweet

caress that promised a fire storm of passion. Everything she did, she did wholeheartedly—from reigning as prom queen to achieving success in the cutthroat broadcasting business. He wanted the pleasure of her passion, hungered for the fervor he knew she would bring to their lovemaking. Wanted to give her pleasure, too.

He speared his fingers through her hair, drawing her closer, deepening their kiss. Tasting her, he savored her unique flavor, the sweetness of mint and feminine heat. He'd been on the brink of arousal all evening and now the ache was pure torture.

"Kim, I want—" His breath came in agonizing gulps, burning his lungs. Barely able to speak, he covered her face with kisses. "Ah, blue eyes...You are so—"

"No. Don't say it." Kim pressed her hand against his chest, feeling his heart beat even faster than her own. "We can't do this. I can't. Not when—" Not when he was so vulnerable, needing reassurance that despite his blindness—temporary or permanent—he was still a man. Not when he still imagined her as she had been months or years ago, before her face had been ripped open. Not when her career had gone up in smoke, a victim of the same earthquake that had scarred her. "If you're going to get well, you need your rest."

He tensed, his fingers still snared in her hair. "You're right, it's probably not a good time."

Heart aching, she slipped from his embrace. Her

lips throbbed with his kisses and wanted more. "I'll be back in three hours."

In the light from the hallway, she saw the tightening around his lips, the frown drawing his brows together. "Sure. I'll be here. I don't have anywhere else to go."

She stumbled from his room. She didn't dare let Jay know how much she wanted him to hold her, love her. If he could see her, he wouldn't question her refusal. Not for a minute. Instead he'd be repulsed. Or worse, he'd pity her. She wouldn't be able to stand that.

Crawling into the narrow bed, she shivered and pulled the musty-smelling covers up over her. For two more days she'd have to keep Jay at arms' length. Then she'd leave, return to the quiet isolation of her house.

And to the desperate loneliness that had begun to seep into her bones.

She balled her hands into fists and gritted her teeth.

No, she couldn't give up. For years her competitive spirit had driven her to succeed in one of the world's most difficult businesses. To lose all she had achieved simply because the world shook for thirty seconds went against the grain.

Somehow she'd find a job that would make use of the talents she had honed since the eighth grade when she'd read the morning announcements over the loudspeaker system at Dana Junior High. She might not ever make it to anchorwoman of a network show, but that didn't mean she had to crawl into a hole.

JAY DIDN'T usually eavesdrop, but Kim had been on the phone most of the morning and his curiosity was getting the better of him. Besides, he didn't have much else to do these days except listen. In fact, last night he should have listened instead of opening his big mouth about how scared he was. No woman wanted a man who was as frightened of the dark as a six-year-old kid.

Leaning against the doorjamb, he pictured her at the kitchen table, the curly phone cord stretching from the wall to the table. He wondered what she was wearing—maybe jeans and tennis shoes because she didn't make much noise when she walked. Denim suited her just fine but he liked her in silk even better—soft and clinging to her curves.

But most of all, he'd like to see her with nothing on whatsoever.

She hung up and evidently spotted him standing by the door. "Did you want something?" she asked, her cultured tone perfect for a TV announcer, an easy-to-listen-to voice that triggered a man's most erotic thoughts.

Jay wanted lots of things, most of which he couldn't have or didn't have the right to ask for. "Just wondering what's going on. You've been on the phone a long time."

"Sorry. I'm probably running up a huge long-distance bill, too. I'll pay you back—"

"I'm not worried about that. I was just—" He jammed his hands in his pockets. "It's probably none of my business anyway. You go ahead with whatever you're doing. I'll just, ah, go wash my car. Maybe I'll take a drive later." He turned to leave.

"I'm job hunting."

His heart in his throat, he whirled back. "You're leaving Paseo del Real?"

"KPRX-TV fired me."

"That's outrageous. They can't do that to you! Why, your news show is the most popular one in the whole county. Your ratings are better than the network programs. They'd be fools to let you go."

"According to the letter I got Saturday when I got home from the pancake breakfast, my personal services contract has been terminated, effective immediately."

Jay found his way across the room and sat down at the table next to her. "Why did they do a stupid thing like that?"

"Probably because they didn't think the viewers would enjoy seeing closeups of ugly red scars on somebody's face." She tried to keep her tone light but Jay could hear the brittle hurt in her voice.

"That stinks. It was their own damn building that fell down on you. If they'd retrofitted the place sooner—"

"But they didn't. And now, unless some miracle happens, I'll never have another on-camera job."

"You can sue them. They can't get away with—"

"Do you know how long they could drag out a suit? And even if I won, it wouldn't change the fact that I'm ugly. A judge wouldn't force them to hire me."

Instinctively, he reached out to her, caressing her injured face with the fingertips of one hand. To him, whatever scars she had were invisible and they always would be—even if he got his sight back. "Sometimes scars take a long time to heal completely. A few more months—"

"I can't believe much is going to change after all this time."

"Maybe a new doctor."

"Actually, I've got an appointment tomorrow in Santa Barbara. A new specialist my mother tracked down."

"I'll go with you."

"You don't have to do that."

"What if you're delayed and it's time for my eye drops? Cat isn't ready to handle the job yet, and you know I can't do it for myself."

Her cheek moved under his fingertips and he knew she was smiling. "I suppose you'll insist upon driving, too?"

"With anyone else, I would. But I trust you not to get us into an accident."

She cradled her face more fully in his hand as if the warmth of his palm soothed her. "I appreciate your vote of confidence."

When, after a moment, she pulled away, Jay thought he'd lost something precious, like a beautiful butterfly who'd briefly landed on his hand only to take flight again.

"So who have you been calling?" he asked.

"Virtually everyone I graduated with who stayed

in the business. Some of them have been quite successful, both with networks and independents. I thought I'd better get the word out I'm in the market for a new job.''

A job that would take her far from Paseo del Real and Jay. With an effort, he swallowed the bitter taste of regret. ''What will you do if you're not...what did you call it? On-camera?''

''Hmm, I'm really good at writing scripts. That's how I got started. I think I'm experienced enough to be a floor director or even produce a show, though I'm not sure anyone would give me a shot at that. Certainly I could arrange guests for talk shows, grunge work like that.''

''But you'd rather be the star.''

''I grew up wanting to be Walter Cronkite, but that doesn't appear to be one of my choices.''

''Thank God,'' he murmured and she laughed, which was exactly what he'd hoped she would do.

He left her to make her phone calls and went outside, although she admonished him not to go far. It was almost time for his next dose of eye drops.

Standing on the walkway in front of his house, he absorbed the heat of the noon sun he could feel but not see. He listened to a bird call, the flight of the bird invisible to him. He knew a neighbor across the street was mowing his grass, both from the scent of freshly cut grass and from the sound, but he didn't know which neighbor was doing his yard work.

He cursed both his blindness and his stupidity for putting his eyesight at even greater risk by playing in the dirt. But most of all, he cursed the fact he couldn't promise to take care of Kim for the rest of her life, promise that she'd never need to work again, that she could rely on him for all of her needs.

And even as those thoughts formed in his head, he knew Kim wasn't that sort of woman. She'd always depend first on herself, no matter who she loved. He just wished he was worthy of being that man.

If it would make a difference, he'd damn well read every book about Saddam Hussein he could get his hands on and take up oil painting on the side. But chances were good he'd only get a gooey mess for his efforts and a splitting headache.

THE RAIN started early the next morning and the sky was leaden for the trip to Santa Barbara, an omen of things to come, Kim feared.

She'd taken the main highway that cut through rolling cattle country to the coastline rather than the winding pass over the mountains, which was more scenic and more of a challenge to drive. But that route could be treacherous when the road was wet.

She found the medical building near the hospital and pulled into a parking space, switching off the engine.

"I'm afraid you're going to be bored to tears waiting for me in the doctor's office," she told Jay as they both got out of the car.

"Don't worry about it. He's bound to have great girlie magazines I can check out."

Her eyebrows shot up. "The doctor's a *she,* so I doubt there will be any girlie magazines to peruse."

"Darn, and I'd been counting on that the whole way here." He waggled his eyebrows and gave her a lecherous grin across the top of the car.

Despite her fears, she laughed as she rounded the car and extended her arm for Jay to take, escorting him toward the entrance to the medical building. He was absolutely amazing the way he could defuse her anxiety with a smart-alecky remark or a quip that seemed to come out of nowhere. Kim had the feeling Jay had missed his calling as a stand-up comic but suspected he was much too serious about himself to have chosen that profession.

WAITING had never been Jay's strong suit. Listening to the quiet conversation in a doctor's office, the hushed tones of the woman behind the counter and inhaling the faint scent of antiseptic soap combined with furniture polish was something he could learn to hate.

He fidgeted in his chair. Hell, he couldn't even pace the room to reduce his pent-up energy for fear he'd bash into the furniture or fall over a waiting patient. He'd give anything to be able to go for a long run along the beach, assuming he didn't get lost in the process or break his neck.

His expensive watch had enough doodads to run a college track meet, none of which he could read, so he didn't even know how long he'd been waiting, and he was damned tempted to rip off the cover, feel the face and find out what time it was. It felt like an eternity had passed.

The door to the back room opened with a creak and the air seemed to warm with Kim's presence like the arrival of the sun after a spring rain. He stood.

"I'm ready to go." Her smoky voice was low and taut, joyless.

"What did the doctor say?"

"I...I'll tell you later."

Her hand trembled as she took his arm and he knew the news wasn't good. She clung to him as they walked down the hallway as if her legs weren't quite able to hold her up. Whatever the doctor had told her had sucked the spirit right out of her. Jay wanted to go back and yell at the woman, force her to find a way to repair the damage the falling light fixture had done to Kim's face, to her life. Unreasonably, he felt guilty he hadn't been there to protect her again, to cover her slender body with his own. To stop her pain.

"Are you okay to drive?" he asked when they reached the car.

"I'm fine."

"We could get a cup of coffee, talk a little."

"No. I just want to...to go home."

His place or her own? he wondered.

He buckled up and heard her blow her nose. She was crying, and he didn't know what to do. Under normal circumstances he'd take her in his arms, console her as best he could. But there was nothing normal about being blind, about being *dependent* on her to do the driving. About not being able to protect her from whatever the doctor had said. Or whatever blows fate intended to hit her with next.

Damn, he felt so useless!

She drove silently, not uttering a word, the only sound the tires on the wet pavement and the slow swish of the windshield wipers. He reached across the car, held out his hand and she took it, her delicate fingers squeezing him tightly. He held onto her the rest of the way to Paseo del Real until she pulled up to the curb in front of his house.

"I'll give you your drops and then I...I need to be alone for a while."

Jay didn't think that was the answer to her problems.

Once inside, he captured her hand again. "The eye drops can wait. Tell me what the doctor said."

"That this, my face, is as good as it gets. Any more surgery would only create more scars." She drew a shaky breath that sounded a lot like a sob. "I'll always be ugly."

"Oh, blue eyes, that's not true." Although she resisted, he tugged her closer, and framed her face between his hands. "Everything about you that matters is beautiful."

"Easy for you to say. You can't see—"

"You're the one who's blind to the truth. Let me show you how truly beautiful you are, Kimberly." He lowered his head, found her waiting lips, kissed her gently, lovingly.

Kim didn't resist. She didn't have the strength to

argue, to warn Jay off, to tell him if he could see the truth he'd never want to kiss her this way. Because, for this moment in time, she needed this man, the feeling that she *was* beautiful in his eyes. She needed his healing tenderness.

She shuddered as he deepened the kiss, using his tongue to toy with hers as his thumbs stroked her temples. Her body responded, warmth spreading through her, heating her skin and making her pliant in his arms.

If he'd pressured her or moved too quickly, she might have had the wisdom to step away, not to cross that final barrier that would change their relationship forever. But the coaxing kisses he pressed to her face, the way his lips skimmed her jaw and lingered at the tender spot beneath her ear lured her into wanting more.

"Let me love you, blue eyes," he whispered.

Beneath her palm she felt his heart beating as insistently as a caller knocking on the front door, and her heart matched his rhythm, pounding against her ribs and pulsing in her throat where he kissed her.

A floating sensation overtook her, as though she were someone else—someone beautiful—and she loosened the top button on his shirt and then another. She slipped her hand inside, palming his muscular chest, his heat radiating through his cotton T-shirt like a furnace turned up high on a frosty winter night. Idly, she again imagined a woman would never be cold sleeping with Jay.

He groaned when her fingers released the top snap of his jeans.

"Oh, baby, I've wanted this for so long. Wanted you."

He lifted the hem of her sweater, pulled it off over her head. Unerringly, he found her breast and suckled her, the sheer fabric of her bra instantly damp, her nipple puckered and aching. With each gentle tug of his lips, her womb responded with a deep clenching.

Suddenly her knees were too weak to hold her upright.

"Jay. The bedroom. Please."

"Yours or mine?"

"Yours. The bed's bigger."

To her surprise, he scooped her up in his arms as though she weighed nothing at all. She wrapped her arms around his neck and buried her face against his shoulder, giving herself over to his strength while she inhaled his rich, masculine scent.

When he set her on her feet beside his bed, it seemed completely natural to slip out of her clothes and watch him do the same. A man moved differently than a woman, even in the simple act of shrugging out of his shirt. Muscles rippled. Skin, taut over sinew, flexed and shifted in a uniquely masculine way.

Because he couldn't see her admiring him, she could give full rein to her examination of his physique, noting the way dark, springy hair swirled across his chest and arrowed lower to form a nest for his arousal. He was a big man, and she was unable to resist cupping him, sheathing him with her hand.

He sucked in a quick breath. "Easy, blue eyes. You do that too much, and this will be over before we get started."

"Then we'd just have to do it again, wouldn't we?" she teased.

With a low, hungry growl, he pulled her closer and she could feel him, amazingly, growing even harder as he pressed against her belly. When had she last felt this feminine? This desirable? Perhaps the answer was never.

With a quick flick of his wrist, he tossed back the jumble of blankets, and brought her down with him across the bed. Intuitively he stroked her in all the ways she liked to be touched, arousing her with hands so expert it was as though they'd always been lovers. Along the sensitive curve of her breast, his palms felt slightly rough. Masculine. And on the tender flesh of her inner thigh, his silken caress abraded her in the most erotic way imaginable.

When he slipped his fingers into her moist heat, she cried out, nearly coming apart in his hands.

"Don't get too far ahead of me, blue eyes, we've only just begun."

"Jay..."

"I know." He covered her mouth with another kiss, determined to continue his braille exploration of every curve and valley of her exquisite body until he knew each inch of her intimately. He cherished the smooth flatness of her stomach, relished the curly hair at the juncture of her thighs that he was sure was the same honey-blond shade as the hair on her head.

Working his way down her legs, kissing, caressing, he reached her fine-boned ankles, like silk over porcelain. He nibbled her toes, massaged her high, proud arches like those of a ballerina. In his imagination he saw her wearing bright pink polish on her toenails, sexy feet in sandals. Even better in his bed.

During the return trip up her legs and beyond, he tasted her heat, drinking deeply while she cried out his name. He inhaled the musky scent of her sex.

Barely able to restrain himself, he rolled away long enough to fumble in the bedside drawer and find a pack of condoms. He ripped the foil open.

''Hurry,'' she whispered, her fingers finishing the job for him, sheathing him.

When he rose above her, she spread her legs, eager for him. He lingered over the excruciating pleasure of entering her, moving slowly, testing his patience. His stamina. His willpower. Until he could no longer resist thrusting into her. Filling her. Claiming her as his own, if not forever at least for today. Claiming his dream.

Kim lifted her hips to meet his thrust, wanting to prolong the exquisite tension building within her. But when he quickened his pace she felt herself rocketing beyond the point of no return. A scream ripped from her throat. She shuddered on the precipice then toppled over the edge, sobbing, wanting him with her wherever the journey might take her.

A moment later, her body still pulsing with its release, she felt a tremor shimmer through Jay, his muscles tensing, and knew he had joined her in going over the top of the world. Only then did he collapse on her, his weight as welcome as though she were an addict who had finally given in to cravings she had denied herself for far too long.

Chapter Nine

The muted daylight in Jay's room had an ethereal quality, as though Kim were in some other, more gentle world that lacked the stark shine of kleig lights. The quiet patter of rain on the roof and the rhythmic dripping from the eaves cocooned them in a secret, private place.

A place she never wanted to leave.

She rested her head on his chest, enjoying the feel of his arm wrapped around her shoulders. During the night, she'd given him his eye drops, except for a few hours of sleep, the only breaks they'd taken from their lovemaking.

Idly she picked up his hand, examining his long, tapered fingers and broad palm that eclipsed hers when she placed them together. A strong hand. A hand that had caressed her, aroused her beyond her wildest imagination. A hand crisscrossed with scars.

"Are all these scars from playing fireman?" She brought the back of his hand to her lips, kissing it tenderly.

"Firefighter," he muttered, correcting her use of

the outdated term. He waggled his index finger, showing her a fine white line on the outside of his finger.
"That one, I was cutting a candy bar to share with
my buddy at the Saturday afternoon matinee when I
was about ten. Had me a big ol' Boy Scout knife that
was so dull it wouldn't cut butter."

"But it cut your finger."

"Bled all over the place. The theater manager gave
me a month's worth of free passes and told me never
to bring a knife in there again. And if I did, I should
cut the damn candy bar on the seat, not in my hand."

"A wise man." Feeling warm and content, relaxed
for the first time in months, she fingered a circular
scar on the back of his hand. "This one?"

"Hot metal. A couple of years ago. A garage went
up in flames and a tank of propane exploded. A piece
of shrapnel caught me. I didn't even know it had happened until the chunk burned right through my
glove."

She shuddered. The gloves firemen—firefighters—
wore were thick. The thought of heat so potent it
would burn through the material gave her a painful,
knotted feeling right in the middle of her stomach.

She kissed the last knuckle on his baby finger, a
crooked joint. "This?"

"Hmm, I was about twelve years old and playing
catcher for a game of street ball. Some kid fired a
pitch at a hundred miles an hour. I didn't catch it
right."

"Fortunate it didn't hit you in the head."

Smiling, he reversed their hands and kissed hers,

lingering, sucking gently on her fingers, first one and then another, drawing the sensation out until her body grew weak with wanting all over again.

"Oh, I got beaned a couple of times," he said, nibbling on her baby finger. "We didn't exactly have helmets in this neighborhood."

"And that's why you're such a crazy man?"

"No, you're the only one who makes me crazy."

He rose up on one elbow and looked down at her, though obviously he couldn't see through his bandages. Still, she could imagine his copper-brown eyes darkening and knew that behind the gauze she'd see a heated look. Just as he would see the same need, as yet unsated, in her eyes.

Was it possible to trust the feelings that were swamping her senses? Emotions that careened beyond simple lust. Their situation was so unusual, both of them wounded. And needy. If circumstances hadn't conspired to bring them together, none of this would be happening.

Was it fate? Karma?

Or simply a moment out of time?

She couldn't help feeling they had nothing in common, no shared interests, yet it felt so *right* to be in his arms. So right to be loving him.

"Kim?" His voice hitched, hoarse and needy.

"We're not done yet, are we?" she asked.

"I'm game if you are."

"I've already noticed you're not a quitter. Under the circumstances, I wouldn't expect anything less than another round." Whatever their reason for being together, she didn't want it to end. Not yet. Though she knew if—*when*—he regained his eyesight, the show would be a wrap. She couldn't burden any man with her ugliness. Nor could she risk seeing pity in his eyes. To prevent that, she'd walk away first.

But not yet. Not today.

For now, the future would simply have to take care of itself.

"After this we might just try it a third time," he whispered. "I understand practice makes perfect." With unerring accuracy, Jay covered her lips with his, taking his fill of her with his mouth and tongue.

He felt as though he already knew her in intimate detail, not just in his imagination but in reality as well. He knew the taste of her lips and the tiny sigh she made when he kissed that sensitive spot beneath her ear. The column of her throat, the slight indentation at the base, was velvety soft, her nipples tiny buds that pebbled under his tongue. His palms caressed her rib cage and smoothed over her slender thighs. She moaned when his hand covered her most intimate place.

He had always desired her. One night of burying himself within her hadn't come close to sating that desire. A thousand times wouldn't be enough.

But he wanted to see her, see her blue eyes darken to violet in response to his touch, see her honey-blond hair spilling across his pillow in wild disarray. Watch her when he entered her. Claimed her as his own. See her lazy smile of satisfaction when he'd brought her to the peak and let her go over the top.

If the earth hadn't slipped off its axis for a scant thirty seconds, Kimberly Lydell would never have been in his arms now. Jay was hard-pressed, even as he slipped into her warmth, to believe the earth wouldn't shake again, setting things back where they had been. Where they belonged. Leaving him out in the cold.

And if he never got his sight back...

Raw, primitive pain sliced through him as though to deny that possibility. His jaw clenched. He thrust into her more deeply, and she surged upward to meet him. His breath came in ragged gasps. Hers did too.

She cried his name as she shuddered, her climax wrapping around him. He drove into her once more before his own powerful release crashed over him.

His strength gone, he buried his head at the juncture of her shoulder and neck, inhaled her sweet scent, and let the darkness overtake him.

A NIGHT of lovemaking had given Kim both an appetite and a glorious sense of being feminine.

"Do you have any onions?" she asked as Jay came into the kitchen, his hair still damp from his morning shower. Shirtless, he hadn't yet snapped the top button of his jeans. In spite of her best intentions, her gaze was drawn to that enticing sight.

No, she didn't want to make love again, she told herself even as the urge fluttered deep in her midsection. For heaven's sake! Never before had she had such an insatiable appetite—a craving for something other than chocolate.

"If I've got any, they should be on the bottom shelf of the pantry," he said, gesturing vaguely toward the cupboard on the left side of the refrigerator where he kept his canned goods. His eye patches were in place over the gauze dressing, making him look like a pirate who had just risen from the sea to capture a wayward ship and ravish every woman on board.

Smiling at the fanciful image, she said, "I thought I'd make *huevos rancheros* for breakfast."

"Sounds great to me. I think we must have skipped dinner last night. I'm starved."

So was she, though she'd willingly forego breakfast for another tumble in bed, she suspected. "I fed Cat. He didn't seem at all pleased we'd forgotten him."

"Not to worry. He could live off his fat for a month and no one would even notice." Running his hand along the counter, Jay found his way to the coffee pot. He poured too much into the mug she'd left out for him and the cup overflowed, burning his fingers. "Damn," he muttered.

She eyed him with concern. "You know, the Braille Institute has some household aids for blind people—"

"I'll have these damn patches off in a couple of weeks. There's no sense to—"

"Your vision could still be impaired."

He slammed his mug down on the counter, sloshing more coffee out of the cup. He whirled toward her, his aim a little off as he appeared to glower at the kitchen table. "My eyes are going to be fine, okay? And I thought you were making breakfast. Unless you want me to do it. I'm terrific with cereal and toast, assuming Cat didn't get into the Cheerios on his own.''

"That's all right. I'll do it." She dipped her head, sorry that the mood of the morning had changed from romance back to reality. Such a stubbornly proud man! She suspected that had been true long before the explosion had threatened to steal his sight.

Opening the cupboard, she knelt and pulled out a plastic bag that contained onions. Studying them, she wrinkled her nose. It was hard to imagine how long the onions had been in the cupboard, an unappetizing combination of sprouted green shoots and black goo. Why hadn't she noticed them when she'd been labeling his canned goods?

Sitting back on her haunches, she said, "I think you're going to have to settle for scrambled eggs."

"How come?" He'd made an effort to wipe up the coffee he'd spilled but as much had dripped onto the linoleum floor as had been swiped into the sink.

"Well, you're either composting penicillin in this cupboard, or aliens have been feeding off these *things* that used to be onions."

He shrugged. "I haven't been doing much gourmet cooking lately."

"Jay—" She stood.

"I don't want to hear it, okay? In another couple of weeks—"

"You need to prepare yourself, Jay. There's no sense sticking your head in the sand. There are ways to cope, to adapt to your…condition. Even if it's temporary. Or, if necessary, for the long term. It would make your life easier.''

He turned away and she saw the tension in his broad shoulders and how his hands curled over the edge of the sink so tightly his knuckles turned white.

Coming up behind him, she linked her arms around his middle and rested her cheek against his back. His skin was hot and smooth, his muscles rippling with tension. She wanted to tell him she loved him, that it didn't matter that he was blind.

But it did matter.

If he could see, she wouldn't have the courage to admit her feelings, these new emotions that had her head reeling. Even now, she wasn't sure that what she was feeling was true and not a creation of her own wants and needs.

But in her heart...

He twisted out of her embrace. ''I've changed my mind about breakfast. I'm going down to the station. They've usually got donuts. Maybe I can get in a workout on the treadmill downstairs.''

''The doctor said not to overdo it.''

''I've gotta stay in shape if I'm going to handle it when I'm back on the job.'' He headed toward the living room but bumped into a kitchen chair Kim had inadvertently left pulled away from the table. He whipped it back into place. ''Dammit, if you leave things lying around I really will break my neck.''

She winced at both the sharpness of his words and his anger. ''I'm sorry.''

He stormed from the kitchen. A moment later she

heard him crashing around in the bedroom and he reappeared wearing a shirt and his dark glasses.

"I'll drive you," she called after him as he went out the front door.

"I'm not a cripple, Kim. I can walk just fine."

She struggled not to be hurt. As gentle as he'd been during the night, as loving, he was as wounded as she. Perhaps more so because he had so much pride. But she couldn't let him ignore the possibility that impaired vision might be with him the rest of his life.

He needed to prepare himself…just as she needed to recognize that being an on-camera celebrity was no longer in the cards for her.

JAY CURSED himself all the way down the block, nearly falling off the curb when he lost count of his steps and reached the end of the sidewalk sooner than he'd expected—*something that wouldn't have happened if he used a white cane, he realized in desperation.*

Kim hadn't deserved his ire; it wasn't her fault his moods were so volatile he was like a dangerous fire, ready to flashover without warning. Spontaneous combustion.

That's how it had been last night with Kim, so hot they'd practically exploded.

Then this morning she'd reminded him of his blindness—that it might not be temporary. And he'd lost it.

Listening carefully for traffic sounds, he crossed the street and turned right towards the station house.

From the feel of the cool air on his face it was still early, the shifts just changing, passing responsibility for the job from one man to another.

He wasn't part of that, maybe never would be again.

The wide driveway dipped in front of the bay doors of the station. He walked a few more paces past the drive, trying to sense where the pedestrian door was. Missing the entrance, he felt his way along the wall, finally grabbing the doorknob and yanking it open.

Most everyone was upstairs. He heard shouting, friendly greetings. Guys kidding each other as A shift prepared to go home and C Shift take over.

It was all he could do not to cut and run. Only his pride, his determination not to quit, kept him walking down the hallway.

He heard Emma Jean's dangling jewelry jingling before she spoke. "Hey, Jay, hon, I had a feeling you'd be coming in today."

"Amazing, Emma Jean, since I didn't know I was coming until minutes ago." He'd rather have stayed at home making love to Kim, but she would have coaxed him into visiting the Braille Institute. He wasn't ready for that yet; that was too much like admitting defeat.

"I was just gettin' myself some coffee. Come on into the office and I'll pour you some."

"Sure, why not?" He didn't have much else to do except hang out with the dispatcher. Nothing useful. No fires to fight, no mountains to climb.

The door opened with a creak and he followed her inside.

"It's going to be a nice, quiet day," she assured him as she placed a mug in his hand.

"What makes you think that?"

"Honey, I'm psychic. You know that. Every day when I get to work I put my palm on that copper shield out front by the door. The way it vibrates tells me what kind of a day it's going to be."

He nodded, although he didn't believe a word of her story, and sipped the coffee she'd given him—hot and potent, the way firefighters liked it.

Emma Jean's chair squeaked as she took her seat in front of the console. "Mrs. Anderson brought in some donuts. They're on the counter if you want one."

He grimaced. "No thanks."

"It's okay. They're store-bought. She said she was going to make some this morning but had an early meeting with the city manager."

"Thank goodness for small favors." Sliding his hand along the counter, he found the cardboard box and selected a donut at random. Gingerly he tasted the sugary frosting. *Huevos rancheros* would have been more to his liking.

At that moment Emma Jean's phone rang. In rapid order she dispatched a rescue unit and engine company from the fire station on the north side of town to a school bus accident before another call came in for Station Six, this one from a frantic wife reporting her sixty-year-old husband was having chest pains.

While Emma Jean was still talking to the hysterical woman, another call came in, forcing her to juggle the distraught wife. A kid at the high school had been experimenting with chemicals in the lab. The explosion wasn't bad, but the whole school stank of rotten eggs.

A warehouse fire came next, three alarms, and Emma Jean dispatched all the available fire trucks in Paseo del Real.

"A quiet day," Jay muttered, amused that Emma Jean's predictions were so blatantly off target—as usual.

She was still answering calls when Jay left the office with his cup of coffee. The station house was quiet now, every vehicle having rolled.

Damn it, he wanted to be out there with them, working the nozzle, taming the beast, dealing with the smoke, the heat. What would he do with the rest of his life if he couldn't fight fires?

Without direction, he walked out of the fire station through the big yawning doors. He could hear another siren, an ambulance maybe, and was drawn to follow the sound in the same way a moth is enticed by the lure of a porch light.

Morning traffic on Paseo Boulevard hummed past him. If he listened carefully he could tell the difference between a pickup and a passenger vehicle. The big trucks were easy, their gears shifting noisily as they lumbered away from a signal.

He stopped at a corner, the traffic light against him

from the sound of the moving vehicles across his path.

But which signal? he wondered, suddenly aware he'd lost his bearings. With Paseo on his right he knew he'd been walking away from the fire station, away from his house. But how far? Had he crossed one street or two while pursuing the ambulance?

At this hour there were few pedestrians. He could probably wave down a car to ask for directions—assuming they didn't run over him first. Or he could bumble his way from one store-front door to another like a senile old man looking for help. A *blind* man who couldn't find his way home.

God, he was tempted to rip off the dressings on his eyes, see for himself where he was. What harm could it do? He'd only need a few seconds to get his bearings. Even if things were a blur, he'd be able to identify something. Wouldn't he?

KIM WATCHED the hands on the kitchen clock tick forward. Jay had been gone for four hours. Past time for his eye drops and no sign of him.

If only he hadn't been so upset when he left; if only she hadn't tried to push him before he was ready to admit he needed help to deal with his blindness.

At first she'd used the time while he was gone to call some friends and associates back east. Now she simply worried.

She didn't dare go after him like a mother tracking down a runaway child. He was a grown man—as he'd so ably demonstrated last night. He knew that he needed his drops. He'd return home in his own time.

Unless he'd been hurt.

Pacing the floor into the living room, she pulled back the lace curtain and peered out the front window. The street was quiet, no cars in view. And no Jay.

Unbidden, the image of Jay lying on the street popped into her head, his lean, hard body battered and bruised by a car he hadn't seen. Hadn't heard. Did he have any ID with him? Would a hospital know to call her? An hour or more ago she'd heard sirens....

Growing increasingly anxious, she went to the phone. She'd call the station. If he was still there, she'd let it go. He'd come home when he was ready.

She picked up the phone and started to dial, then stopped herself. She didn't want whoever answered the phone—or Jay—to think she was keeping track of him.

It would be better if she drove by the station, just happened to drop in. Maybe she'd spot him walking home and he'd never know she'd been out looking for him.

The decision made, she grabbed her purse, the bottle of eye drops and went out the door. Minutes later she had circled the block twice without seeing Jay and had parked her car across the street from the fire station. The big doors to the garage were up, the fire trucks gone.

Did she dare go inside? The man should have enough sense to know when his medicine was due.

Still, unable to see, he might not know what time it was.

Or maybe he was laying prostrate on a treadmill in the basement of the place with no one around to find him.

Slipping out of the car, she crossed the street and entered through the door leading to the dispatcher's office. It was oddly quiet. Her tennis shoes squeaked on the hardwood floor as she walked down the hallway. At the door marked Dispatch, she stopped, opening it.

Emma Jean looked up and grinned. Her dark hair looked like she'd run it through an egg beater, her cheeks were flushed. "Hey, hon, has this been a heck of a morning or what? I knew the minute I woke up today that it would be a doozie!"

"I've heard a lot of sirens," Kim conceded.

"Tell me about it. I've rolled equipment from every station in town and finally had to ask for mutual assistance from Arroyo Grande for a brush fire up north. Awesome!" Despite her glistening cheeks and the dark eyeliner that had run, Emma Jean looked as though she'd just won a marathon race.

"I was, uh, looking for Jay. Did he drop by?"

"Yeah, hours ago." The dispatcher frowned. "He's not back home?"

Kim shook his head.

"I saw him leave. I mean, I thought he left. I was as busy as a flea on a hot frying pan, but I could have sworn he left the station." She shrugged. "You could check his quarters upstairs, or maybe he's down in the workout room.''

''Thanks. I'll do that.'' Except the doctor had told Jay to take it easy. And a quick tour of the rooms upstairs didn't turn up anyone.

Truly worried now, she wandered back outside. How far could he have gone? She considered the Smoke Eaters Bar and Grill, but according to the sign she'd seen on the door the bar didn't open until noon. Not knowing what else to do, she got back in her car and began to cruise the neighborhood.

If he'd been run over, she rationalized, someone would have called the paramedics, who would have recognized him. Emma Jean would have known if he'd been injured. But where—

As she turned yet another corner onto Paseo Boulevard, she saw him.

Sitting on a bus bench blocks from home.

A wave of relief washed over her, easing the tightness in her chest, and she felt an upwelling of love so potent she could barely suppress it.

She pulled the car up beside him and rolled down the window on the passenger side, his glum expression making her heart go out to him. ''Need a ride, mister?''

His head snapped up. ''You always go around picking up grumpy old men?''

''Only when they're exceptionally good looking.''

He nodded, rising slowly as if he were carrying a heavy burden, and got into the car. ''I was wondering if you could take me to the Braille Institute.''

Unable to speak because of the emotion clogging her throat, she reached across the car and took his hand. Only a very courageous man could admit his weaknesses.

Chapter Ten

"We're here," Kim said as the car slowed to a stop.

"You know I hate doing this." He hated the need to be here. Hated being blind. And more than anything, he hated that he'd gotten lost and had been too afraid of risking his eyesight further by lifting his bandages. Or too terrified he'd see nothing but darkness even without the gauze protection and patches.

"Think of it as a field trip. Those were always my favorite classes at school."

"Right," he grumbled.

"In addition to being legally absent from school all day, when we got back to class we had to write a report. Naturally, I excelled at that."

He fought the urge to smile. "Why am I not surprised?"

"Of course, I dragged the whole writing process out so I'd be excused from math class the next day— which is something I truly loathed, to my parents' everlasting dismay."

He did smile then. Hard not to when Kim was so

damn cheerful about her own shortcomings. "About my foul temper this morning—"

"Don't worry about it, Jay. It's only natural to be angry when fate dumps on you. I didn't take what you said personally."

Releasing the seatbelt, he turned to face her. The perfume she was wearing today made him think of a sultry Caribbean night with flowers blooming everywhere. "What about you? Were you angry when the doctors said they couldn't fix your face?"

When she didn't immediately respond, Jay cursed himself for having mentioned her scars at all. She probably didn't want to think about her injuries any more than he wanted to confront his blindness, temporary or otherwise.

"Furious!" she said in a harsh whisper as though the pain and anger were still near the surface. "The one thing I had going for me was reasonably good looks, and poof! My whole career drops into the trash can."

"You've always been more than just a pretty face." Instinctively, he reached out to touch her and discovered she was wearing her scarf again. He tugged the silk fabric out of the way, caressing her cheek with the back of his hand and finding she had on glasses—dark glasses, he imagined, dramatic ones with rhinestones. Or classic round ones that would make her look studious. "How 'bout we forget this Braille Institute business after all and make out right here in the car?"

Beneath his fingertips, her cheek shifted with a smile.

"And you've always had the makings of a rogue." She patted his thigh, dangerously close to a part of his anatomy that had already begun to react to her nearness. "Come on, hotshot. We've come this far. Let's go see what these folks have to say for themselves."

Kim got out of the car and walked around to the other side, offering Jay her arm in order to guide him from the angled parking space into the Institute, which occupied a converted two-story Spanish-style house on the outskirts of town. The red tile porch and big double-door entrance looked inviting. Beside the door was a discreet plaque identifying the organization both in raised bronze letters and smaller braille characters.

"There are three steps up to a porch," she warned him.

"Great. I'll try not to fall over my own feet."

"Relax, Jay. I imagine you wouldn't be the first person to stumble on these steps and probably not all of them have been blind."

"Sorry. Maybe I should have brought Buttons along and signed him up for guide-dog lessons."

She elbowed Jay in the ribs, smiling despite herself. The more anxious the man got, the more he tried to make light of the situation. Perhaps she should develop the same coping mechanism to deal with her problems. After all, she could easily switch careers to modeling scary Halloween costumes.

The receptionist looked up as they stepped into the lobby, her extraordinarily thick glasses catching the glint of the overhead lights. Large, bold-print letters filled the computer screen beside her desk.

"Hello, there. May I help you?"

Kim suspected they were little more than moving shadows to the receptionist, whose desk plaque identified her as Sherry Summerland, but the young woman's smile brought a special radiance to the room.

"I had an accident a couple of weeks ago," Jay said. "And I've been having problems with my, uh, eyes."

"Can you see at all?"

"I, uh, I'm wearing patches. The problem's supposed to clear up in a couple of weeks."

"Of course, I understand. Once a week we have an orientation class that can help with mobility and an adaptive cooking program—"

"I don't think I need a class. By the time I took the class, I'd probably be able to see just fine."

Realizing Jay was backpedaling from the reason they'd come to the Institute, Kim said, "We were just planning to check out what programs you have available now and then perhaps later—"

"Later I'll be fine."

"As I recall," Kim continued, "you have a small store with useful items for those who are visually impaired."

"We do indeed." The young woman tilted her head. "Your voice sounds very familiar, miss. Quite distinctive but I can't quite place it. Have you been in before?''

"Two or three years ago I did a story on—"

"Oh, my gracious, you're Kimberly Lydell of KPRX. I listen to you on TV all the time. You're my favorite newscaster."

"Fans fall at her feet wherever she goes," Jay said under his breath, a teasing smile in his voice.

She punched him with her elbow again. "That's very kind of you to say, Sherry. I'm glad you enjoyed the program."

"Oh, yeah, you're terrific, but I've missed you lately. Did you get changed to the morning show? I don't get up so early, you know. I don't have to be here until nine and still I'm in such a rush I never have the time to watch TV." She picked up the phone on her desk and spoke to someone on the intercom, announcing Kim's presence—and her status as Paseo del Real's most popular newscaster.

"I'm not actually on-air any longer," Kim tried to tell the receptionist, but it was too late. From every direction, staff members began appearing in the lobby, ostensibly with other business to conduct but all of them glancing at Kim, even those with severely limited vision.

She ducked her head and shifted her scarf to cover her shattered cheek although, rationally, she knew most of the employees wouldn't be able to see her clearly, much less her scars.

Finally, Eric Robinson, the director of the institute appeared with his guide dog, Sage.

"Ms. Lydell, it's good to see you again."

She shook his extended hand and made introductions, briefly explaining the situation. Within minutes, Eric had swept them into the room off the lobby that served as a store for adaptive equipment.

"Now then, what can I entice you with?" Eric asked. "A talking watch? Very helpful for the visually impaired."

"I don't need—"

"It's not very expensive, Jay. And I was worried you wouldn't know when to—"

"Okay, okay."

She frowned at him. Jay was suddenly beyond grumpy, absolutely bristling about something. Oddly, this time she didn't think it had anything to do with his temporary blindness.

Eric worked his way down a glass-top counter, running through an entire catalog of adaptive equipment for both home and office.

When Jay gave no indication of interest in anything, Kim said, "The liquid-level indicator would be good. You burned your fingers on the coffee this morning."

He grumbled his agreement.

The man's mood had definitely gone from glum to morose and Kim wondered what had set him off this time.

"What about a Scrabble game with raised letters?" she asked. "We could play—"

"You'd wipe me out, blue eyes. How 'bout the cards instead? You ever play poker?"

"Well, no, not really."

"Great. Put 'em in the shopping cart, Eric, ol' buddy."

Eric didn't react to Jay's rude tone, simply setting the cards aside and moving on.

"We have a folding white cane that is quite practical," Eric said.

Tension radiated from Jay, his fingers flexing into fists, a muscle twitching in his jaw. "I don't want a white cane."

"That, of course, is your choice," Eric said smoothly.

Kim didn't like the feel of this whole situation, and it was Jay who was behaving out of character. "We'll take the watch, the level indicator and the cards, Eric. Maybe later we'll come back for some of the other—"

"Over my dead body," Jay muttered.

As quickly as she could, Kim arranged payment and shooed Jay out the door. In the parking lot, she whirled on him and jabbed him in the chest with her finger.

"What the *hell* was going on in there between you and Eric?"

"Eric?" he mocked, sing-songing his name. "How old is that guy, anyway?"

"Maybe forty, I don't know. What's his age got to do with anything?"

"He's in love with you, that's what."

Her jaw went slack. "You're kidding."

"He's slick, honey. Maybe you didn't notice but

when you're blind you hear stuff in a person's voice. And what I heard is that guy is hot for you.''

She rolled her eyes. ''He's *married,* Jay. He's wearing a ring. Last I heard, he had a couple of kids.''

''So? That didn't stop him from falling all over himself trying to make points with you.''

''Oh, for heaven's sake!'' She'd never expected that Jay would be jealous of any man. He was too macho, too confident of himself. Except, at the moment his lack of sight had undermined his usual buoyant self-confidence, she realized.

Standing on tiptoe, she placed a kiss on his lips. ''Even if Eric weren't married, I'd never even notice him if you were within a thousand yards.''

His arm snaked around her waist, pulling her close. ''Then trust me, blue eyes, I'm not going to be out of your sight anytime soon. Sure as hell not while Eric is anywhere on the continent.''

Despite his foolish jealousy, Kim thrilled to Jay's promise. It wasn't necessarily realistic, not when he couldn't see what she'd become since the earthquake. Even so, she cherished the sentiment. A woman needed to hear of a man's devotion from time to time.

''Could we go home, sweetheart, and take up where we left off last night?'' he asked. ''Before I turned into a grouch this morning.''

''An excellent idea, Mr. Tolliver. One I was considering myself.''

She leaned into him, accepting his deepening kiss, and suspected dinner would be a little late tonight.

"IT SEEMS TO ME in strip poker you have all the advantages," Kim complained, shivering. She was already down to her bra and panties. Only Cat, who had taken up temporary residence in her lap, was keeping her warm. The clothes she'd pulled on following a lazy afternoon of lovemaking were now neatly folded on the floor, the dirty dishes from the dinner she'd cooked scattered across the kitchen counter. So far Jay had only discarded his T-shirt, which left her with an enticing view of his well-muscled chest.

A woman could easily get used to spending her days—and nights—like this, she thought with a pleasurable smile. They might not have much else in common, but they certainly were compatible in bed.

Jay leaned back in the kitchen chair, holding his cards close to his chest. "What makes you say I've got an advantage?"

"Well, first of all, you cheat."

His eyebrows shot up. "*Moi?* Are you impugning my honor, madam?"

"Every time you deal, you cop a feel of those cards with the raised numbers and suits so you know what I've got."

"A mere slip of the fingertips, I assure you. It's beneath a man's dignity to cop a feel—" He waggled his eyebrows. "Unless it's a beautiful woman."

She swallowed another grin. "Then you make up the rules as we go along. Whoever heard of one-eyed Jacks and eights being wild, anyway?"

"Dealer's choice. An ancient card-playing custom."

"Yeah, but when I get a one-eyed Jack, then you tell me deuces are wild."

"So I'm a little indecisive. A man has a right to be ambivalent when he's trying to get a woman naked and back into bed with him."

"Again?" She laughed. "Don't you ever wear out?"

"Not where you're concerned."

She was about to admit her stamina was doing just fine, too, when the phone rang.

He answered, listened a moment, then passed the phone to her. "I think it's your mom," he said.

Stunned, she took the phone. "Mother? How on earth did you find me here?"

"It wasn't easy, my dear, but I must say Councilwoman Anderson was quite helpful. When you didn't return the messages I left on your machine, I became concerned. Since Evie is such a good friend of Chief Gray—"

"I'm sorry. I haven't been home for a couple of days."

"I see." Disapproval lowered Dr. DeMille-Lydell's voice to an accusing tone much like that she'd use to announce to an entire class of graduate students that they had failed their final exams. "We had hoped you'd call after you saw the doctor in Santa Barbara."

Kim felt a stab of guilt. She *should* have called, or at least arranged for call-forwarding, but other more pressing matters had intervened. Namely, making love with Jay. "There wasn't anything to report, Mother." At least not on the medical front.

"That's regrettable. We had hoped…" She hesitated. "Nonetheless, I am surprised you have moved in with that…fireman."

"Firefighter. And he needs to have drops put in his eyes every few hours…." She glanced at the clock over the stove and realized that, distracted by the game of strip poker, she was late giving Jay his medicine. "It seemed more reasonable to stay here for a day or two rather that drive back and forth all the time."

"Yes, well, I'm sure you've thought it all through. I needn't be the one to remind you that you have a spotless reputation in this community and some very high standards to maintain. Living with a man—"

"I'm not *living* with him, Mother." Not exactly. "And, no, you don't have to remind me about my reputation." Which, until very recently, would have been that of a beautiful professional woman who was far too busy for any kind of a relationship. Now, ironically, she was ugly with enough time on her hands to play strip poker with the sexiest man she'd ever known.

"Mother, I've got to get back to—" She grinned as she thought about her state of undress. Better not to go into details.

"Of course, dear. But do keep us informed of any changes."

After a promise to do just that, Kim managed to

hang up. She turned to Jay. "It's past time for your drops."

"Does your mother disapprove of all the men you see, or is it just me?"

"Well, she was very fond of a neurosurgeon I was dating a year or two ago."

"Yeah, I bet." He shoved back his chair, stood and paced to the refrigerator. Opening the door, he pulled out a bottle of beer.

"Of course, she didn't know Gregory was a closet gay or she might not have been quite so excited about the prospect of me marrying a doctor."

Jay whirled around. "My God, how did you find out?"

"He told me. He's a really nice guy and the perfect date. No groping under the table, no *copping a feel*," she emphasized. "No awkward moments at the front door. I really enjoyed his company."

Twisting open the bottle of beer, he glowered at her. "Dare I ask what happened to this fantastically perfect relationship?"

"He found someone special and they moved to San Francisco. I got a card from them at Christmas. They're very happy together."

"And I'm happy for them." Jay's shoulders visibly relaxed. "Anybody else in your checkered past I ought to know about?"

"None that I can think of at the moment," she said brightly. "No secret vampires or married men slipping out on their wives. Typically, my social life has ranked somewhere between boring and deadly dull."

He set his beer aside. "Why don't I see if I can change that for you?"

"Does this mean I've lost the game?"

"Nope. It means we're about to try out a new set of rules. You wanna be on top this time?"

Anticipation rippled through her. She lowered Cat to the floor. "Actually, I've always wondered what it would be like showering with a man, and you've got quite a large—"

Before she could finish her thought, Jay had pulled her to her feet, wrapped his arms around her, and lifted her. "Consider it done, blue eyes. Last one into the tub has to scrub the other guy's back."

JAY TOOK all the time he could loving Kim, holding himself back as long as possible, memorizing every sweet curve of her slender body, lingering over every taste. Savoring the moment as the water that pelted them chilled and they moved from the bathtub to his bed.

Even as they exploded together in an earth-shattering climax, he was afraid this would be the last chance he'd have to hold her. He'd been acting the fool, sticking his head in the sand, ignoring reality.

Hell, reality scared him to death. Blindness. Losing Kim.

Knowing that she was too good for him.

Finally, he lifted his weight away from her and rolled to the side, pulling her with him. Damn, she felt so good, so right in his arms. But it wasn't gonna happen. Not with the prom queen and the guy from the wrong side of the tracks—blind or not.

If nothing else, her mother's phone call had made that abundantly clear.

But he was damn well going to enjoy Kim as long as he could.

ALEX WOODWARD, the president of KPRX-TV returned to town at the end of the week. Kim was his first appointment. Having watched Jay's courage at the Braille Institute—however reluctant he'd been to face that his blindness might be permanent—she was determined to confront the man who had so thoughtlessly fired her without giving her an opportunity to appeal his decision. She at least deserved her day in court.

Early that morning, she left Jay snoring in bed, dressed in her most professional outfit and drove into town. Following the earthquake, KPRX had moved their studios and offices to a new three-story building, one that lacked any particular personality but that apparently was sturdy. Antennas sprouted from the top of the structure like quills on a porcupine's back.

Uneasy about seeing her friends, Kim went directly upstairs rather than dropping by the studio. Harriet motioned for her to go right into Mr. Woodward's office. Squaring her shoulders and holding her chin high, Kim stepped through the double doors.

"Kimberly, so good to see you." Standing, Woodward buttoned his pinstripe suit jacket and rounded his desk, extending his hand. "You're looking wonderful."

She forced herself not to flinch under his all-too-careful scrutiny as she shook his hand. Although she'd arranged her hair in a soft fall over her left cheek, she knew her scars were still visible. But she refused to turn away.

"Thank you, Alex, it's good to see you, too."

He ushered her to a corner grouping of comfortable chairs that had a view out the window of Paseo del Real and the coastal mountains in the distance. A large man, he'd always dominated a room with both his size and his blustery personality. But now age spots were beginning to appear and the bags under his eyes were deep enough to pack for a weekend trip.

"How have you been feeling?" he asked as he filled the chair opposite her with his bulk.

"Quite well." An active love life did seem to buoy her spirits. "In fact, I had planned to call you about coming back to work when I got your letter. Frankly, I was a little shocked you hadn't had the decency to fire me in person."

A flush stole up his cheeks, deepening the fine web of veins that were already too apparent, a result of too many three-martini lunches.

"You know how this business is. You're up one day and then the next—" He shrugged. "Regrettable, but a necessary part of broadcasting. I'm sure you understand—"

"No, Alex, I don't. It was your building that collapsed on me. I would have thought—"

"Actually, that's not quite true. We were leasing the building and therefore our liability is limited. You might want to have your attorney talk to the building owner. I'd be happy to give you his name and address, although I understand he lacked adequate insurance and has already filed for bankruptcy."

Thus far she hadn't considered suing anyone. Now it was too late. "What I want is a job."

He fumbled in his inside coat pocket and pulled out a cigar, which he rolled between his fingers like a man who had been told by his doctor not to succumb to temptation. "Have you seen Tiffany Lane, our new anchorwoman?"

"A time or two." Kim hadn't been impressed. Tiffany seemed bright and shining but lacked substance.

"Wonderful girl. Lovely, really. Did you know she has network experience?"

"No, I wasn't aware of that." Unkindly, Kim suspected Tiffany must have been fired from the network or she wouldn't be working at KPRX. Or perhaps, Kim realized with a start, Tiffany was the leverage to get a network's attention in order to sell the station.

"Yes, indeed. Extremely well respected in New York. Extremely. We're lucky to have her in Paseo, truly fortunate."

Kim wasn't all that sure the viewers were pleased, but she hadn't been given a vote. "Alex, I'll be honest with you. I understand my scars prevent me from ever doing on-camera work again. But that doesn't mean I can't do something for the station. This is my hometown, after all. I know the people, what they care about.''

Stuffing the cigar back in his pocket, Alex stood and paced across the room to his desk. He wiped his palm over the top of his thinning gray hair, finally settling in his leather swivel chair.

"I'm sorry, Kimberly. Really I am. But you may have heard we're in negotiations with one of the networks. The details are all hush-hush so far, but it's crucial our payroll is kept under control. You can understand that, can't you?''

Kim didn't want to beg for a job. She'd never had to before, although landing an on-air position had never been easy. But she'd gotten no more than social calls back from her contacts across the country. Apparently ugly anchorwomen weren't in high demand at the moment for any kind of television work.

She swallowed her pride. "I'll work for less. I write good news copy, Alex. You know that." Dammit, in addition to local issues, she knew more about international news and the big financial markets than anyone else in Paseo. Her stories always had a bite and were based on solid facts she'd researched herself. Finding a local hook was her forte.

He actually hung his head like a contrite little boy. "I'm sorry, Kim. Right now there simply isn't a spot for you on the team. Perhaps later…''

Team! That was a load of crock. Alex Woodward ran the organization like a tyrant.

Under other circumstances, Kim might think she

was well rid of him and KPRX-TV. There'd be other opportunities to pursue.

But not now. She was fast running out of options. Soon, she'd be running out of money, too.

Chapter Eleven

After the disastrous interview with Alex Woodward, Kim drove around town for a while. Until that blasted earthquake she'd been able to solve her own problems. Now she felt helpless. For the first time in her adult life she wanted to lean on someone.

Inevitably, her route took her back to Jay's house.

He met her on the front porch. Though he was still wearing his eye patches, and would be for another week or so, he no longer needed regular eye drops. Still she hadn't brought herself to move out, shuttling instead between his house and hers for clean clothes.

He hooked his arm through hers before she even got in the door. "We're late."

"Late? What's wrong? Where are we going?"

He hustled her down the porch steps. "Emma Jean called. It's a command performance. You want me to drive, or should we walk?"

Kim had come to Jay's house to cry on his shoulder and whine about her uncertain future. Now her head was spinning. Jay had a way of keeping her off balance and, in the process, raising her spirits.

She shook her head in bewilderment. "We'll walk while you tell me what's going on."

"It's Chief Gray's sixtieth birthday and our beloved Councilwoman Anderson baked him a huge sheet cake." With Jay striding along the sidewalk so confidently, Kim was hard-pressed to keep up in her high heels. "Emma Jean wants everybody there so we can distract Mrs. Anderson long enough for the bakery to get a substitute cake to the station."

"What kind of distraction does Emma Jean have in mind? Starting a series of brush fires?"

As if his vision were twenty-twenty, he gave her a sharp glance through his reflective sunglasses. "I don't think so. She's probably going to read palms, or something. Nobody will be able to resist hearing her predictions—and guessing how far off she is."

"Sounds reasonable." Although Kim could only hope there wouldn't be a rash of emergencies in town during the next hour or so—or however long it took to bake and decorate a cake then get it delivered.

"So how did your talk go with your boss?" Jay asked.

"Ex-boss."

"That doesn't sound good."

"He wasn't even interested in hiring me to scrub toilets. Not that I lowered myself far enough to apply for the job, but only because I didn't think of the idea at the time."

"I keep telling you, with your sexy voice you'll find something."

"Like what? Replacing Emma Jean as dispatcher

when the councilwoman finds out her birthday party for the chief has been sabotaged?''

''Hey, if Mrs. Anderson knew Emma Jean was saving her bacon when it comes to the chief, she'd probably have the city council give her a commendation.''

Kim supposed that was a possibility, though she'd be reluctant to bet on the outcome. Despite her eccentricities, Mrs. Anderson was a strong-minded woman and was on the boards of directors of half the nonprofit organizations in town, from the battered women's shelter to the local university. Not many people in Paseo del Real would be willing to cross her.

A little breathless when they reached the fire station, Kim led Jay in through the open bay doors. All the fire trucks were parked inside without a firefighter in sight. Apparently Emma Jean had rejected the notion of brush fires popping up all over town.

''Where is everyone?'' Kim asked.

''Let's check dispatch first. If they're not there, they'll be upstairs in the dining hall.''

They discovered the C-shift crew plus department secretaries crowded elbow-to-elbow in the dispatcher's office paying homage to Emma Jean's gypsy blood, violin and concertina music piped in over the loudspeakers.

A burst of laughter came from the room when they arrived. Emma Jean was busily dealing a deck of cards on top of her console with the man Kim remembered as Mike Gables watching avidly.

''Come on, Gables, admit it!'' one of his buddies

shouted. "You bribe some woman to bid your price up at the bachelor auction every year just so you'll keep your studly reputation intact."

"Not a chance, Strong," Mike countered, grinning over his shoulder. "Besides you're the one who pays your sister to open the bidding so damn high when you start strutting your stuff."

"Me?" Logan Strong, tall and lanky and quite handsome in his blue uniform, laughed. "Couldn't be me. I don't even have a sister."

"The cards don't lie," Emma Jean insisted, defending her prediction. "The queen of hearts is right there. She tells me Mike will claim the highest price at the next bachelor auction...and it will be the last time he is eligible to participate."

Everyone hooted and hollered, and Mrs. Anderson, who was squeezed in behind the dispatcher's chair, beamed a smile at Chief Gray. "Perhaps someone will pay a higher price for a more mature man—someone like Harlan."

The chief's face turned bright red. "Now Evie, I'm too old for a bachelor auction. That's for the young guys."

Evie clearly didn't agree with Harlan's assessment. "Nonsense. Besides, we older women have more disposable income to spend on what interests us. We can always outbid the younger girls if we're taken with a man—all for a good cause, of course."

At that moment, it looked as though the chief would have welcomed a five-alarm fire.

Tactfully, Evie Anderson suggested they all go upstairs to enjoy the birthday cake.

"Wait a minute," one of the secretaries piped up. "First you have to tell Tommy's fortune, Emma Jean."

The shy youngster was shoved forward, his face even brighter than the chief's. "Come on, guys. I don't wanna have my fortune told."

Emma Jean snatched the boy's hand, making a big production of reading his palm. "Ah, yes, I see great wealth and a long life. And *love!*"

"Hey, maybe we ought to get the girls to bid on Tommy," somebody suggested.

Shooting a plaintive look at his friends, he snatched his hand back from the dispatcher and stuffed it in the pocket of his raggedy jeans.

Kim's heart went out to the youngster, and she was ready to add her vote to ending the poor boy's ordeal.

The chief, apparently agreeing with Kim, said, "Gentlemen, I think we've had enough—"

"No, not yet!" someone shouted in another desperate effort to delay the unveiling of the sham birthday cake, which apparently hadn't arrived yet. "Jay's here. How 'bout telling us his future?"

Eager hands grabbed at Jay, pulling him farther into the room. Through a break in the crowd, Emma Jean caught Kim's attention and winked at her.

Unwilling to be the victim of the dispatcher's false predictions, an anxious feeling curled through Kim's midsection.

"I don't have to check Jay's palm to predict his

future,'' Emma Jean said to the crowd, her dark eyes flashing with amusement. ''I'd bet my crystal ball he's not going to be eligible for any bachelor auction this year. Marriage is definitely in the air.'' With laughter and good humor, everyone in the room turned toward Kim.

She ducked her head, looking away. Emma Jean shouldn't have said that. Once Jay got his sight back he'd have no interest at all in marrying her, no matter what Emma Jean's crystal ball or Jay's palm might say. And how awful it would be if they did marry while Jay was blind. Everyone would pity him, thinking she'd tricked him into marriage without him realizing how terribly scarred she was.

Even if her heart did overrule her good reason, what would they do when the sensual spark wore off? What would they talk about? However enticing the idea might be, no married couple could spend all of their time in bed.

No, marriage wasn't in the cards for Kim—probably never—and certainly not with Jay. She'd never take advantage of him that way. She'd leave first.

Dear heaven, the thought of walking away from Jay was as painful as having the lighting fixture fall on her again. But that's exactly what she'd have to do— walk away.

And soon, she realized with a start.

The deeper, the more intimate their relationship became, the harder it would be on both of them when the time came. Kim couldn't delay that moment much longer. Only until his bandages were removed, she told herself.

One way or another, by then she'd have to go.

Behind her there was a disturbance and a firefighter leaned into the room, whispering in Kim's ear, "Give Emma Jean the all-clear signal, would you? The bakery cake is in the station."

Within moments of Kim catching Emma Jean's eye again, the crowd broke up. Kim was swept along upstairs with the others, where everyone joined in a rousing chorus of "Happy Birthday" to the chief. Once the cake was cut, Harlan looked relieved, excusing himself as rapidly as politeness allowed.

Kim found herself standing next to Evie Anderson while Jay was across the room laughing with his buddies. Looking at him, she wished she could go home with him right now, curl up in his arms and forget that what they'd had together these past few days couldn't last forever.

"Looks like my birthday surprise was a success as far as the firefighters are concerned," the councilwoman said, noting the way the party guests had made short work of the cake. "There have been times when I thought these young men didn't appreciate my home cooking."

Disguising a smile, Kim forked another bite of the store-bought cake into her mouth. "Oh, I'm sure they do." The bakery cake was quite good. Clearly it hadn't had time between the oven and the fire station to dry out, and the baker had followed the recipe, not substituting salt for sugar.

Sighing, Evie looked off into the distance. "I seem to have lost my ability to attract a man in my old age. Harlan's so sweet but so much of the time he seems, well, to want to avoid me."

"He hasn't been widowed very long. Maybe he's worried that if he expressed an interest in another woman, he'd feel disloyal to his wife."

"It's been three years. And at our age—" Evie set her thin lips in a determined line. "There's still some life in these old bones and I don't intend to squander a minute of the remaining time I have."

Taking a deep breath, Kim decided the councilwoman had to be told the truth, or at least part of the truth. "Well, then, perhaps it's your perfume that's keeping the chief at a distance, Mrs. Anderson."

She looked at Kim, startled. "My perfume?"

"It's a little strong." Downright potent, as though Evie had a lilac bush strapped to her back. Evidently her head injury had affected both her taste buds and her ability to smell.

A frown pinched her brows together. "Ever since my concussion, it's so hard to tell. I try not to overdo it."

"In this case, I think it would be better to err on the safe side and not use perfume at all."

Distraught, Evie nodded. "Thank you, my dear. Honesty has always been something I admired in you, even when you were doing controversial stories about our community. You were, if nothing else, absolutely fair to both sides."

"Thank you."

"Will you be going back to the news show soon? I believe KPRX has missed your integrity on their newscasts recently."

"Not enough that they plan to hire me back. Because of my scars, I'll never be on camera again." The admission hurt more than Kim had realized it might. Briefly, she told the councilwoman of her meeting with Woodward that morning, concluding with, "...and so I'm unemployed and hunting for a job anywhere I can find one."

"Gracious, it was dreadful enough that you were injured, but to lose your job, too." Evie patted Kim's hand affectionately. "Well, you have spirit, my dear. I'm sure you'll find something, though if you leave Paseo it will be our loss."

"You're kind to say that, Mrs. Anderson."

"Kind? Bah! Haven't you heard I'm the mean ol' witch on the council who won't let a bunch of liberals spend the city into the poorhouse?"

"I have heard something like that, yes," she admitted, laughing. Mrs. Anderson had rounded up community opposition to more than one program Kim had supported, and in the process had swayed her fellow council members to vote with her. But she'd always done her homework and her votes weren't outlandish. At least not usually.

Evie smiled conspiratorially. "We're just going to have to see what we can do to keep a fine young woman like you in our community. Our city needs spirit like yours. Of course, if Emma Jean is right in

her predictions—'' she glanced across the room towards Jay, ''—you'll be highly motivated to stay.''

Kim struggled to speak past the lump in her throat.
No one could understand what an impossible dream
that was. All these years Kim had concentrated her
efforts on her career, thinking marriage and family
would come later. Love could wait.

Now it was too late.

Although Jay claimed her scars didn't matter—and
the people in this room didn't appear to find her re-
pulsive—the rest of the world wouldn't be that kind.
She'd seen enough faces turn away from her to know
the truth. She was desperately ugly.

In time, Jay would know that too. The reality of
living day to day with a disfigured woman would
wear on him. Make him question his choice. Under-
mine whatever feelings he had for her.

She couldn't stand that. She'd rather have her heart
ripped out and thrown in the trash than see regret or
pity in his eyes.

JAY HAD lost track of where Kim was. He was standing with Mike Gables, their backs to the kitchen
counter, and Mike had been waxing on about C shift's
rescue of a couple stuck in a car that was dangling
half off a freeway overpass a hundred feet in the air.

Though firefighting ''war'' stories were entertaining, at the moment Jay wasn't all that interested.

He tilted his head, listening for Kim's voice, but
the crowd was so noisy he could barely hear himself
think. Inhaling slightly, he tried to catch the faint

scent of her perfume. All he got was a snoot full of lilacs, as if some heavy-handed probationer had gotten carried away with spraying designer room freshener around the place. It really stank.

"Don't sweat it, lover boy," Mike Gables said. "Your girlfriend is still here."

Jay snapped his head back toward Mike. "I wasn't worried about—"

"Yeah, right. You were craning your neck around trying to figure out if she'd left yet. I thought for a minute you were going to snatch off your eye patches and take a look for yourself."

Jay shrugged. "Maybe." He sure as hell was getting sick of being in the dark.

"You going to get your patches off pretty soon? With you off the job, I'm pulling too many double shifts and it's playing hell with my social life."

Jay laughed, knowing darn well Mike wouldn't let anything, including work, interfere with his active bachelor's life for long. Emma Jean had been one-hundred-eighty degrees off base suggesting Mike would be getting married anytime in the next year— probably not within the next decade. She'd been equally wrong about Jay's chances for marriage.

"I thought you'd already broken every heart in Paseo," Jay said, trying not to think about Kim and how she was the only woman he'd even consider marrying. And she had always been out of his league. "There can't be many females around who you haven't loved and left just when they had visions of standing at the altar with you."

"I leave 'em real happy, ol' buddy, and never any-where near the church door. It's a matter of principle with me that I never lead a woman on. A few good times, a bouquet of flowers, a bottle of wine and some sweet words, but *no* promises."

"I'm sure they're all grateful for that."

"So when will you know if your eyes have healed okay?"

"I'll know the verdict in a week." Seven days until he learned whether or not he'd be dependent on others for the rest of his life. That jarring thought turned the bakery cake to acid in his stomach.

Jay started as a cold, damp nose slid into his open palm.

"Hey, Buttons. How have you been?" He scratched the top of the dog's head and gave him a couple of solid pats on his side. "Been to any good fires lately?"

"No, but he sure does make a hit with the school kids who come here for field trips," Mike said. "He'd make some family a great pet."

"Probably better than a guide dog." Then again, maybe Buttons liked that job, too. "See you later, Gables."

Taking Buttons by the collar, Jay ordered, "But-tons, find Kim."

To his delight, the dog took off right across the crowded room, Jay at his side hanging on tight. "Coming through, folks. Coming through."

Everyone chuckled but it was Kim's come-hither

laughter floating across the room that drew Jay to his destination.

"I DON'T THINK I'm going to be very good company," Kim said as they walked up the block to Jay's house. A niggling sense of depression had settled over her now that the distraction of the chief's party had passed. "Maybe I ought to go on home. I'll come by tomorrow—"

"Hey, we'll have none of that. If you're feeling down about Woodward and KPRX, I've got great shoulders to cry on—as well as other interesting body parts."

All of which looked particularly appealing in a tight-fitting polo shirt and jeans, she mused.

"There's nothing much you can do," she said. "I need to update my resumé and figure out what to do next."

"So I'll come with you. I'll check out your etchings while you do whatever it is you have to do."

Halting on the sidewalk beside her car, she slanted him a look. "Sculptures. I work in clay but they're nothing special. Strictly amateur."

He slid his hand to the back of her neck, capturing her when she would have turned away. "It's not good to be alone when you're feeling down, Kim. I know. Let me come with you. I'll stay out of your way, if that's what you want. But I don't want you to be all by yourself. Not today."

She lowered her head and he pulled her into his arms where she could rest her head on his shoulder.

She forced herself to swallow the sob that threatened. "I've always known just where I was going and now…I'm lost, Jay. I don't know what comes next." Never had she been so vulnerable, so at a loss.

"Then why don't we stick together? Maybe we're going in the same direction."

Kim didn't dare allow herself to believe that was possible. But in spite of what she'd said, she didn't want to be alone, either. Not just yet.

"Okay, you can come up to see my etchings. But if you start raving that I'm the most talented artist you've ever known, I'll know you're not only blind but a liar."

"Considering I've never known any other artists, I figure you're a shoo-in for the top spot. But if you want to lie and say you're not quite up to Picasso's standards, it's all right by me."

Laughing, she shook her head. "Guess again. Picasso was a painter, not a sculptor." And Jay was a man with the uncanny ability to lift her spirits simply by being himself.

KIM'S HOUSE was big.

Jay could sense the space all around him as she walked him through the carpeted rooms and out onto the deck where her heels clicked on the wood flooring.

The scent of oak trees washed clean by the recent rains hovered in the air along with a faint trace of sea salt drifting in from the distant ocean. And her own floral perfume. Jay inhaled deeply, mentally separating the scents until hers was the only one that mattered.

"This is some kind of place," he said, envying her. He'd always lived in town, in the same little house a block away from the busy traffic on Paseo Boulevard. "It must be wonderful living out in the country."

"I love it and I'd hate to have to sell—"

"Hey, don't give up so easily. You've only been unemployed a week."

"Tell that to my bank account," she said grimly. "Buying this place was a stretch for me, maybe too big a stretch in retrospect."

"You'll work something out."

"I hope so." Her sigh was long and troubled. "I'll show you my studio, if you want. Then I'm going to go change into something more comfortable."

"Hmm, that sounds like even more fun." He waggled his eyebrows. "You need any help?"

"Jay, you're impossible! Don't you ever think of anything beside sex?"

"Nope. Not when you're around."

She left him alone in the studio, the smell of dust and clay all around him. He wouldn't be able to tell good art from a piece of junk, even with a fully functioning pair of eyes. But as he ran his fingers over a sculpted figure he sensed her touch. The way she'd molded the clay with her hands. Held it. Caressed warmth from a lifeless form.

A fawn nuzzled beneath its mother, suckling while it stood straddle-legged. The instinct to protect her offspring was apparent in the doe's alert stance—head up, sniffing the air for danger.

Suddenly, Jay pictured Kim protecting *his* child, holding the baby in her arms, *his* child suckling at her breast. The image, the yearning, struck him so powerfully it nearly brought him to his knees.

What if he'd already gotten her pregnant? Condoms weren't one-hundred-percent safe. Would she even want to have his baby? How could he convince her—

"Don't look so grim," she said from somewhere nearby, laughter in her voice. "I told you I was strictly an amateur."

Only then did he realize how tightly he'd been clasping the sculpture of the doe and her fawn. Relaxing his grip, he set it back in its place, but the image of Kim holding his baby remained achingly vivid in his mind's eye.

"I think I've found the answer for all your problems," he said.

"Is that so? I can hardly wait."

"It's pretty simple, really." If things were different, marriage to him would be a simple solution. Except he was blind and wouldn't be able to support her or the baby that had sprung to his mind. "You can start showing your etchings around town, someone will discover your artistic talents, you'll be an overnight success and your pieces will sell for millions."

Chuckling, she came up beside him, slipping her arms around his waist. "I had no idea what a vivid imagination you had."

He hugged her close. "Trust me, sweetheart. You haven't even begun to fathom what my imagination can come up with."

URGENCY FEULED Kim's lovemaking that night. The hunger to feel she was whole in his arms, not scarred. Not lacking in any way. The prayer that in a perfect world their differences would evaporate, become meaningless.

She'd never made love in her own home before. In a way she had trouble articulating, bringing Jay here meant he'd crossed an invisible barrier. He was the first who had breached the walls of her solitary castle.

Wanting to recall every tactile sensation of loving Jay, her hands caressed him, learning the sharp details of his face, testing the strength of his shoulders, measuring the corded length of his forearms. Perhaps later she would sculpt him from memory, lovingly turning a mound of clay into the image of this man. But it would never be enough—only a pale imitation of the original.

When the discordant ring of the phone woke her the next morning, she relinquished the comfort of Jay's warmth reluctantly. She rolled over, the chill air raising goose bumps on her bare flesh, and picked up the instrument.

Chapter Twelve

"Jay, wake up!" So excited she could barely breathe, she shook his arm.

Rolling over, he snared her by the hand and dragged her back under the covers. "I *am* awake. Who could sleep with all that racket going on?"

"Then you heard?" She tried to struggle free, but he didn't let her go, capturing her instead against his long, hard body.

"I heard, but I don't know what KUCP is. It sounds like a bad case of stomach flu."

"Oh, Jay, it's so wonderful." Laughing, she quit fighting him and instead covered his face with a dozen kisses, relishing the feel of his rough morning whiskers on her cheeks. "KUCP is the public radio station at the university here in town. They play classical music—"

"Ah, that's probably why I've never heard of 'em."

"—and they have a nighttime call-in talk show on public affairs with guests and everything. They want to interview me for the host job, Jay! Me! For public radio.''

''That's great, blue eyes. How'd they know you were job-hunting?''

''I don't know. I forgot to ask.'' She'd practically forgotten her name, she'd been so surprised by the call.

''I figured all along you'd be snapped up in a hurry as soon as the word got out that KPRX had dumped you. Maybe all those calls you made helped.''

''Maybe, but it's not a done deal yet. They've got to have dozens of applicants for a job like that, even if it doesn't pay all that well, which it probably doesn't given the limited funding for public radio. I was too excited by the call to ask about the salary, either.''

''My money's on you.''

She scooted off the bed and out of his reach, glancing at the clock. ''I can't believe how much I have to do before this afternoon. That's when Mr. Abbott wants to see me, at three o'clock. I've got to get my hair done. My fingernails, too. And I really should study up on classical music.''

Sitting up in bed, Jay yawned and ran his hands through his sleep-mussed hair. ''I thought the show was about public affairs?''

''It is, and I've been so wrapped up in my own problems lately—including hanging around with a certain firefighter,'' she said with a grin, ''that now I need a crash course in the headline news, too.'' Hastily, she grabbed up some clothes and headed for the shower. "But Mr. Abbott might ask me something about who my favorite composer is. I ought to be prepared."

"Tell him Aton Pederisky. I think he wrote reggae music for Bob Marley in the eighties."

"There isn't any such composer. You're just making that up." She gave Jay a whack on his leg as she passed by his side of the bed. "Besides, KUCP doesn't exactly play that kind of music."

"Come to think of it, Aton was a probie when I started in the fire department. Even so, a little reggae would be good. You could start a new tradition. Liven up your late night with Lydell."

"Hey, I like the sound of that, and I don't mean reggae," she called over her shoulder as she stepped into the bathroom, closed the door and grinned into the mirror for the first time in months. "'Late Night with Lydell.' That really does have a nice ring to it." It might not be network television, but it was a job and a new beginning.

Jay leaned back against the padded headboard of the bed, listening to the shower running, and imagined warm water sluicing over Kim's smooth, perfect shoulders. He knew she would land the job at KUCP—her voice, her experience, everything about Kim made her perfect for the job. She'd be staying in Paseo del Real and that made him glad.

But she wouldn't be needing him any longer. She was back on her feet, or would be soon enough. He was still stumbling around in the dark. Even when he could lose his patches, the situation wouldn't change no matter how good his eyesight.

He swore succinctly under his breath.

What would she want with a man who didn't know Bach from Beethoven, the Mideast from the Far East and Picasso from nobody?

Getting out of bed, he found his clothes on a nearby chair and pulled them on. At least being a firefighter had taught him to be neat about where he dumped his gear. The last thing he needed when the fire bell sounded was to be fumbling to find his boots and turnout coat in the dark.

Minutes later, Jay caught the scent of steam mingling with the honeyed fragrance of Kim's shampoo as she came out of the bathroom.

"Oh, you're dressed." He listened to her move around the bedroom, pulling back the curtains, opening the closet door. "What do you think I ought to wear for the interview?"

Nothing at all, would be his preference if she were interviewing with him. But then, for what he had in mind, he'd hire her sight unseen.

"You used to have a blue sweater with kind of a rolled-up collar and you wore it with beads or something. You looked dynamite in it."

"You remember that?" He heard her surprise. "I probably haven't worn that sweater in a couple of years."

"It's the kind of sweater a man wants to get his hands on." And take off as soon as possible. "Besides, it matches your eyes."

"You're certainly observant."

He smiled, slow and sexy. "The devil's in the details, they say."

"Yes, well..." He heard her rummaging in the closet. "The sweater might be too casual. I've never met Mr. Abbott. What do you think about chic professional?"

"I think he won't be able to resist hiring you no matter what you're wearing."

He felt the swift brush of her lips across his. "Thanks. When my nerves turn into a solid rock in my stomach this afternoon, I'll try to remember that. God, I hate interviews."

"You'll do just fine. Trust me."

Like a dandelion seed caught on a current of wind, she sailed away from him. Desperately, he wanted to catch her and bring her back. Not just for now but forever.

That thought startled him. He'd never considered *forever* with anyone—he hadn't actually thought it was possible. Now he discovered he'd been right all along.

"You want to borrow my safety razor while I fix us some breakfast?" she asked.

He swallowed the bitter taste of regret. "Thanks but I'll wait till I get back to my place. I've never been particularly fond of slicing my throat first thing in the morning."

That's exactly what Jay felt was happening. No matter how happy he was for Kim and her prospects for a new job, her good news sliced across his heart.

Sure, the cut wasn't deep—he'd bleed slowly. But soon the reasons they were together would drain away. Things would go back to the way they'd been before the earthquake. Wrapped up in her new career, she'd have no more need for him. Meanwhile, unless his luck turned rotten, he'd have his sight back and wouldn't be dependent on anyone.

Then he would go back to being just one more guy in her unseen audience who became aroused every time he heard her low, sexy voice.

IDLY, JAY FINGERED the raised numbers on his watch, counting the minutes since Kim had dropped him off at his own house and driven off for her interview.

He hadn't been able to sit still so he'd walked to the fire station. Engine 61 and the paramedics had been out on a run and there wasn't much going on, so he parked himself in the driver's seat of the classic fire truck out back. From the smell of things, Tommy was up to his elbows cleaning grease off the engine.

"How'd you get her to talk to you?" Tommy asked.

Jay turned his head in the kid's direction. "Who?"

"That foxy lady you've been hanging around with."

Kim, of course. She'd made a hit with all the men at the station; a fifteen-year-old boy would be no exception.

"Actually, she showed up at my house on her own one day. I think she'd decided I needed some rescuing."

"Oh." The boy sounded disappointed.

"You got some girl in mind you'd like to talk to?"

"Maybe."

Jay could almost hear the kid's shoulders lift in a shrug of mock indifference. A sure sign of adolescent hormones not knowing quite what to do with themselves. In high school Jay hadn't had enough money to date so he might not be the best person to be giving advice. But Tommy didn't often ask for advice; Jay had to give it his best shot.

"Is she in any classes with you?"

"Yeah. Algebra."

"Why don't you volunteer to help her with her homework?"

"She's smarter than I am."

"Hmm, serious problem. Guess you'll have to ask her for help then."

"Then she'd think I'm a stupid dweeb."

Fiddling with the gearshift, Jay gave that one some thought. "Not necessarily. I mean, girls kind of like it when a guy can admit he's got weaknesses. You know, all that macho stuff can get old. If you picked a really tough question—maybe one of those extra-credit things teachers are always handing out—she'll think you were pretty smart to even come close to getting an answer, but she'll realize you don't necessarily think you're perfect."

Metal clanked against metal while Tommy considered Jay's idea. "What would I say?"

Mentally, Jay rolled his eyes. This kid was terminally shy! "Let's see, you should try to catch her right after class so you can walk down the hall with her while you talk. Then say something like, 'Hey, did you try such-and-such problem? That one was really hard, wasn't it?'"

"What if she didn't try the problem?"

"Well, then..." Jay hadn't known scripting a romance would be this tough. "Suggest you try working it out together. Let her know you think she's real smart."

"She's awesome. Blows away every test."

"Great. Then show her you're not intimidated by her brains."

"I guess...." Another whiff of grease cleaner rose in the cool afternoon air.

"Does this girl have a name?"

"Yeah. It's Rachel. Her dad owns a '67 Mustang with a built 350 and duel carbs. Balanced and blue-printed. The whole nine yards. Totally awesome!"

Jay grinned to himself. Apparently Rachel's brains were only part of the attraction.

Fingering his watch again, Jay wondered how long an interview could take. Maybe he ought to head on home—

He heard the clicking of heels on the concrete and lifted his head.

"Jay!" Kim called to him, her footsteps all but running. "When I went by the house and didn't find you, I thought maybe you'd be here. It's so exciting—oh, hi Tommy—Mr. Abbott asked me to be the guest host for tonight's show. Sort of an audition. I've got to get to the library to do some research and then I need to make a ton of calls. You know, line up a few guests I can talk to on the air and let them respond to call-in questions. Assuming anybody's listening, of course. It's awfully short notice—''

Jay climbed down from the fire truck expecting Kim to eventually take a breath and let him get a word in edgewise.

''—to get anyone on air from back east—they've probably all gone home from the office by now—and it would really be the middle of the night there when we're on the air, but I should be able to get some local experts. Maybe someone on oil pollution along the coastline, what it's doing to the birds and water-fowl, that sort of thing.''

''Just what a person with insomnia needs to put them to sleep,'' Jay suggested mildly.

''Not too titillating, huh?''

''Probably not on Howard Stern's list of hot top-ics.''

''Well, this *is* public radio.'' She sounded only slightly affronted by his suggestion. ''I don't want to be too outrageous.''

Instinctively, he reached out to her, caressing her face with his fingertips. ''Honey, just listening to you is all the titillation I can handle, whatever topic you come up with. You'll be great.''

''I hope so.'' She brushed his lips with a quick kiss. ''Anyway, I wanted to tell you I won't be back until late. Can you fix your own dinner?''

''As I recall, there's still about a month's worth of chili con carne in the cupboard. I'll handle it.''

"Good. You need a lift home?"

He shook his head. "I can find my way."

"Wish me luck, then. 'Bye, Tommy, good to see you again."

Her high heels clicked a retreat back to the street. A moment later, the familiar sound of her car engine started, and quickly faded away.

"Man, that is some foxy lady you've got there!" Tommy said in awe.

"Yeah, she is that, my man." But she wasn't *Jay's* foxy lady...and very likely never would be.

STATION KUCP had a pipsqueak of a signal but Jay found it just as Kim's voice announced, "Good evening, Paseo del Real. Welcome to the first, and I hope not the last, edition of 'Late Night with Lydell' on KUCP, your public radio station. I'm Kim Lydell, your host for the evening, and I think you're going to find tonight's show fascinating. For our first hour we're going to be talking about the art of dance—"

Jay groaned. Oil spills might have been more interesting.

"—and with us via the phone are two experts. One is the world-renowned ballet director of the San Francisco Ballet Company and the other is one of his protegées, a young woman who gave up the ballet stage to become one of the most noted striptease dancers in the Tenderloin area of the same city. We'll be right back after these announcements—"

Jay burst out laughing. Damned if she hadn't come up with something titillating after all!

Lying down on the couch, he stacked his hands behind his head on a pillow and settled down to listen to the premier edition of "Late Night with Lydell."

A moment later, Cat joined him, his purr growing in volume as Kim began to introduce her guests.

WOMEN WERE supposed to glow when they perspired; for the past three hours Kim had sweated from every pore in her body.

With a silent sigh of relief, she announced that KUCP would be airing uninterrupted music till dawn, switched off her mike and leaned back in her chair. Unlike at KPRX-TV, there were no directors or producers on hand, only the station engineer, Joe Montoya. He gave her a boyish grin and a thumbs-up through the glass partition.

"How do you think it went?" she asked the young man, her adrenaline still speeding through her veins. She hadn't done any radio broadcasting since her college days and had been rusty on the equipment. But Joe had covered for her when she'd almost disconnected a caller.

"Hey, you were great. Your lead-in had me hooked right from the top."

Thanks to Jay not letting her get away with a dull story.

Kim did think her first segment had gone well. Finding a former ballerina who had turned burlesque dancer because as a single mother she couldn't earn enough in ballet to make a living, had led right into the topic of adequate funding for the arts. Certainly a subject suitable for public radio, not at all outrageous. Kim might have exaggerated just a tad in the opening to call her guest a stripper—and burlesque *was* suddenly experiencing a resurgence of popularity—but the interview had seemed to flow nicely.

Each of the next hour-long segments featuring guest experts on the recent coup in Indonesia and a specialist on techno-stock purchases, Kim considered adequate programming for such short notice. She'd do better next time. Assuming she got a next time.

Shoving back her chair, she stood. Her shoulders and neck ached, her blouse was damp and stuck to her back.

"I wish we'd gotten more calls."

Joe was shifting things around his control panel, setting up the next tape for the all-night show. "Your five calls are practically a record. We don't exactly have a big audience, you know."

"I know." Still, in some magical way she'd hoped for more interest from whatever audience they had. *She'd hoped Jay would be one of her callers.* Which was an unfair thought. Funding for the arts and military coups probably didn't hold his interest long.

She picked up her purse and dropped the pen she'd used to take notes into the side pocket. "I don't know who told Mr. Abbott I was job-hunting, but I'm sure glad they did. I'd really like to land this spot." Facial scarring didn't show on the radio. No one would care what she looked like, only whether she did a good job of attracting an audience.

"I was in Abbott's office last night. I couldn't help

but overhear Councilwoman Anderson talking to him. I mean, it's not like she even knows how to whisper.''

Kim laughed. That was true enough.

''I think I heard her mention your name.''

''Really?'' Kim knew Mrs. Anderson had connections at the university, but she'd seen her only yesterday at the chief's birthday party. If she worked that swiftly at everything she did, Harlan Gray was definitely in trouble. ''I'll be sure to thank her when I see her again.''

''I think Abbott's the one who ought to be thanking her.'' A surprising blush stained his cheeks. ''I could listen to you talk all night.''

Pleased with his approval, she slung her purse over her shoulder. ''Well, I'm off, Joe. Thanks for your kind words and for keeping me on track tonight.''

''Wait a sec and I'll walk you out.''

''You don't have to.'' She'd parked right behind the building. ''I can find my way.''

''It's part of campus security, ma'am. Women aren't supposed to walk alone after dark.''

''Good point.'' Although she wished Joe hadn't called her ma'am. He wasn't *that* much younger than she was, maybe in his early twenties and still in college. Somehow his gesture of respect made her feel ancient.

She waited patiently for him to walk her downstairs and safely out to her car. Once he had, she thanked him and drove off. The streets of Paseo were eerily deserted at this hour, the stores dark. Even the big gas station at Paseo and Broad Street was closed.

She considered going back to her own house. But her nerves were still jittery, her body filled with unspent energy.

Darn it all! Foolish or not, she wanted to be with Jay.

The lights were off when she arrived. Of course, there wasn't much point in him turning them on, since he couldn't see, but she worried he was asleep. Maybe he hadn't even listened to the show. She didn't want to wake him.

Quietly, she slipped into the house. The streetlight cast the darkened living room in faint shadows. One of them moved, forming itself into the shape of a broad-shouldered, lean-hipped man.

"Hey, blue eyes. You knocked 'em dead."

Hearing his praise made her spirits soar. "You listened?"

"Sure I did. What guy wouldn't want to check out a stripteaser?"

She eased toward him. "Burlesque dancer. Very high class."

"A single mother making it on her own. Good for her."

She slipped her arms around his midsection and rested her head against his chest. He had listened and cared. A commentator couldn't ask for much more than that—except a larger audience.

"We didn't get many calls." *You didn't call,* she wanted to say.

He nuzzled his cheek across the top of her head and his hands stroked down her back. "Some of us guys were too busy listening and fantasizing about you to pick up the phone.''

''From a professional perspective,'' she whispered, wanting to purr like a kitten, ''I shouldn't come between the audience and my guests.''

''Trust me, nobody will mind.'' His hands covered her buttocks, pulling her closer. ''I don't know about you having a night job, though. Might cut into your sex life.''

''Da boom-boom-boom, da boom.'' She gyrated against his arousal, stripteaser style. ''Or make it more interesting.''

Groaning, he scooped her up in his arms, and Kim was confident there was no better way in the world to expend surplus adrenaline than by making love with Jay.

Chapter Thirteen

"I don't know about you, but I'm going stir crazy." Kim rinsed her coffee cup and set it on the draining board to dry. She and Jay had slept late that morning. Since then she'd paced the floor waiting for a call from Mr. Abbott, knowing full well it was too soon for the university to have made a decision. Twice she'd checked to make sure she'd arranged call forwarding correctly—cursing her thrift for never having purchased a cell phone she could carry with her. Then she changed the message on Jay's answering machine in case she missed Mr. Abbott's call altogether.

"Why don't we get out of the house for a while?" she suggested.

Jay shoved back his chair from the kitchen table and picked up his empty cereal bowl. "Great. We can go bowling. There ought to be open lanes this time of day."

She scowled at him. "Beyond the fact you can't see the pins, you're still supposed to be taking it easy." Though as she thought about it, Jay was amazingly athletic—and adventuresome—when making love. For that matter, she'd surprised herself in that regard, too. No wonder she'd slept so soundly.

"Okay, let's go to the beach."

"Evidently your new watch doesn't have a calendar function. It's still early spring."

"That's the best time for walking along the beach. No crowds. No pretty girls in bikinis distracting us serious guys from—"

"Right. There are no girls because it's *cold* at the beach this time of year."

"It's not raining, is it?"

"No," she admitted. "In fact it's sunny."

"Perfect. Get your jacket, and we'll go by Vince's Deli, pick up some sandwiches and pop and have a picnic. It'll be great."

Lacking a better idea, Kim agreed. It might indeed be relaxing to stroll along the beach. At least she'd stop staring at the phone, willing it to ring, and get her mind off her troubles. Jay probably needed a change of pace, too. Only a few more days until he'd learn if the explosion had blinded him or permanently impaired his vision; a few more days until he'd see her scars for the first time. Unless she left first.

A sick feeling filled her with dread. What would she see in his eyes the first time he looked at her?

After showering, she dressed casually in jeans and tennis shoes, applied her makeup lightly and was ready to go. Wearing cutoffs, a stenciled T-shirt and ancient running shoes without socks, Jay was waiting for her.

Unerringly, her gaze was drawn to his muscular

legs roughened by a light furring of brown hair. "You'll freeze without long pants," she pointed out.

"Naw. If I get cold, I'll go for a run to warm up."

"I hope you don't expect me to keep up with you."

"Only in bed, blue eyes. Only in bed."

That she could do—with pleasure.

She drove them to Vince's Deli, a hole-in-the-wall shop a block off the main thoroughfare in the heart of the business district. Two glass cases displayed a variety of cut meats, pasta dishes and salads. A half-dozen round tables provided limited seating, but most of the business was takeout. They were too early for the lunch crowd, so the deli was empty.

Guiding Jay through the maze of tables, she stopped at the counter and looked up at the sandwich selections posted on the wall. "Let's see, they've got turkey, roast beef, meatball—"

"I'll have pastrami on a roll with extra mustard. Vince has got the best pastrami in the county—guaranteed—and mustard so hot you taste it all the way down."

"Okay, I'll have the same."

His head swiveled in her direction. "You like hot mustard?"

"Sometimes. According to my mother, it's a throwback to my peasant ancestry. She insists it's gauche to disguise perfectly good food with spicy condiments."

Jay laughed. "Then I must have peasant stock on both sides of my family tree. As far as I'm concerned, catsup, mustard and hot sauce are the three major food groups.''

Kim chuckled. She had seen him doctor his food more than once and been concerned he'd added too much hot sauce. But he'd never even blinked.

An elderly man appeared from the back room. Barely taller than the glass case, he had white hair, angular features and a hooked nose so large it looked too big for his narrow face.

''Jay, my boy! Where you been keepin' yourself, eh? You don't like deli no more?''

''Hey, Vince. Yeah, I still like deli. I've been busy is all.''

Jay reached across the counter and Vince took his hand in both of his, lowering his voice. ''I heard on the news about your eyes, son. You gonna be okay?''

''No sweat, Vince. I'm gonna be fine.''

Vince shot Kim a curious look. ''Busy with this pretty lady, I betcha. No time for your old friends, eh?''

''I'm here now, aren't I?'' Jay introduced Kim briefly. ''We want two of your best pastrami sandwiches on buns with double mustard, okay?''

''You got it, son.'' Vince went busily to work slicing buns and layering mustard, pickles and pastrami on the bread but it didn't slow down his ability to talk. ''You know, when this boy worked here I couldn't keep enough pastrami on hand. I swore he kept hiding it in his hollow leg and takin' it home to his mama.''

Jay laughed. ''I ate every bite, Vince.''

''You worked here?'' Kim asked.

"Among other places."

"He was the best worker I ever had," Vince insisted. "Made deliveries, swept out the back room, worked up front here at the counter, and never a nickel missing from the till. Not ever. Can't get help like him no more. Boys ain't interested in working. They just wanna loaf on the job."

Kim imagined Jay had never loafed a day in his life, until recently, and then not by his own choice. It had to grate on him terribly to have his activities so restricted. To feel suddenly useless.

Vince placed the two wrapped sandwiches on the top of the counter. "You know, lady, you catch this boy and you'll have a good one. No grass growing under his feet. He'll always be able to provide for his family. He's a firefighter, you know that?" He spoke with such pride, he could have been Jay's father.

"Yes, I know. He rescued me."

"That a fact? Well, then…" Vince glanced from Kim to Jay and back again and smiled broadly. "He'll take good care of you, you'll see."

Kim ducked her head to shield both her discomfort and her scars. She shouldn't allow Jay's friends to think their relationship was a permanent one. Building a lifetime together based on hot sex and spicy mustard would be courting failure even if he could deal with her scarred face.

JAY DIRECTED her to one of his favorite beaches not far from Avila where the cliff gave way to a sandy stretch rarely frequented by tourists.

''There ought to be a dirt pullout along here,'' he said. ''Big enough for maybe two or three cars.''

''I see it.'' The car bumped as it eased off the road into the dirt. ''We're pretty high above the beach here. How do we get down?''

''There's a path and stairs. I'll show you.''

She switched off the engine. ''Why does that sound like it's going to be the blind leading the blind?''

''Damn, I didn't know you were blind, too. I never would have let you drive.''

She gave him a stinging shoulder punch, and he laughed.

A strong, steady wind blew in from the Pacific, catching Jay full force as he got out of the car. They were near a point of land here, unprotected from the elements until they descended to the horseshoe-shaped beach below.

He hooked his arm around Kim's shoulders and tried to get his bearings from the feel of the wind in his face and the sound of the waves rolling against the beach down below. Her floral scent, the feminine slope of her shoulder distracted him, and he had to redouble his efforts in order to concentrate at all.

''That way,'' he said, pointing. ''There ought to be a couple of big boulders about two feet apart right on the edge of the cliff. They mark the top of the path that leads to the stairs.''

''If you say so.''

''After my mother got real sick, I used to bring her down here. She couldn't make the climb down to the beach and back up again so we'd sit on those rocks and eat our lunch. She said just being here made her feel better.''

"You were very close to your mother, weren't you?"

"We only had each other. Before she got so sick—" His voice caught on the memories, both good and bad. "I suppose I used to envy kids who had dads and brothers and sisters, but I never doubted for a minute that Mom loved me. She would have taken a bullet for me, if she'd had to. I would have done the same for her.''

But there hadn't been any way for Jay to make her well. He'd had to watch her weaken and her condition deteriorate one day at a time, year after year, although her spirit never faltered. Not until the very last. He'd never forget her courage. Kim had shown the same determined bravery the night she'd been trapped by the earthquake.

"Come on, let's see if we can find us some abalone shells on the beach. I used to have so many, my mom finally said it was them or me. There wasn't room in the house for all of us.''

"I used to collect shells. I don't know what happened to them, though.''

"Well, then, we'll start a new collection for you.'' And maybe whenever she looked at the shells they found today, Kim would remember him and how good they'd been together.

When Kim spotted the path Jay had been talking

about and the steep steps to the beach, she didn't want to consider how they'd get back up to the road. Little wonder his mother had stayed at the top.

"Use the railing," she warned when they reached the stairs. The sand that had blown across the steps made them slippery.

"Okay, I'll slide down the—"

"Jay!" She grabbed for him before she realized he was only pretending to slide down the railing. She groaned and leaned her head against his shoulder. "You and your stunts are going to be the death of me."

"I certainly hope not," he whispered, rubbing his cheek against the top of her head in a sweet caress.

When they reached the beach, he took her hand, swinging their arms together as they walked side by side.

A rocky point of land blocked the wind here, calming the air and smoothing the waves as they rolled against the shore. Sunlight glistened off the water making starbursts dance on the cresting waves. With each footstep, Kim sank into fine-grained sand.

"I wish you could see this, Jay. It's a beautiful day."

He pulled her around, tugging her closer, and cupped her face with his free hand. "Another couple of days and then I'll drink in my fill of all I've been missing."

She knew he was talking about her, not the ocean view. "You might decide you're better off keeping your blinders on."

"Not a chance."

They walked to the edge of the water where the sand was hard-packed then turned west along the curving bay. The gentle breeze toyed with her hair, flipping errant strands in front of her face. She curled them back behind her ears.

"Wait a minute. There's a shell." Dashing forward a few feet, she knelt and dug into the sand, pulling up a perfect abalone half shell. The outside was rough, the inside as smooth as polished stone, the white alabaster glistening with a rainbow of colors.

She brought the shell to Jay, holding it like an offering. "Feel. It's flawless."

His big, strong hands enclosed both the shell and her own hands. He ran his thumbs across her wrists. "As smooth as glass but warmer. Absolutely flawless."

Heat sped to the pulse point he had caressed; her skin warmed. "I'll keep it forever."

Dipping his head, he kissed her. His cool lips molded to hers, his tongue plunging inside as she opened for him. His taste was as elemental as the sea, as addictive as breathing. How could she walk away from this man she craved so deeply?

How could she not?

Aching with indecision, she slipped the shell into her jacket pocket. A precious memento of their day together.

A CHILL FOG drove them from the beach in late afternoon following their picnic lunch. Puffing and panting, Kim made it back up the path to the road and decided she really needed to get into a fitness program. Sitting around reading news copy all day was not conducive to building muscle mass. In fact, the mass was probably settling in her thighs. Rock-hard they weren't.

To her surprise, her sister Leanne's BMW was parked outside Jay's house when they got home, her willowy sibling just walking down the porch steps.

After telling Jay they had company, Kim got out of the car and waved. "Hi, Leanne."

"Hi, midget. I was looking for you."

Kim winced at her old nickname. She couldn't help it if Leanne got all the tall genes along with the brains in the family. "Is something wrong?" she asked when they met on the walkway.

"Not that I know of." Her gaze slid to Jay, who was getting out of the car.

"Then mother sent you to check up on me?"

Leanne lifted her slender shoulders. She had beautiful features she rarely exploited to best advantage—striking golden-blond hair she hid by pulling it back in a casual twist at her nape, high cheekbones that would benefit from a touch of color and a dynamite smile she camouflaged beneath a serious, academic demeanor.

"She's worried about you," Leanne said.

"More like she's worried about what I do affecting her reputation in the academic community."

"Give her more credit than that, Kim. She may not

have the most innate mothering instincts in the world, but she does love you.''

''I know.'' Though it did hurt from time to time to be the least-favored daughter.

Jay joined them on the walkway. ''Is this a family meeting or can anyone join in?''

Kim introduced Jay to her sister, who extended her hand. When he didn't respond, Leanne glanced at Kim, obviously embarrassed she hadn't realized—or had forgotten—that Jay couldn't see her, his wide aviator glasses a perfect disguise.

''Mother sent her to check up on me,'' Kim explained to Jay.

Leanne recovered from her slip. ''*And* to let you know she heard you were on KUCP last night. She wishes you'd told us so we could have listened.''

''The opportunity came up suddenly. I was so busy organizing guests for the show, I didn't think about letting anyone know.'' Even now, she wasn't sure her parents would care.

''Kim was terrific,'' Jay said. ''That stripteaser she interviewed had me on the edge of the chair.''

Leanne's naturally arched brows rose. ''Really?''

Leaping in to avoid a misunderstanding, Kim said, ''The show was about the lack of adequate funding for legitimate dance programs like the San Francisco Ballet.''

''Oh. I was actually hoping you'd found a way to liven up KUCP's programming.''

''Maybe, if they hire me—''

''Why don't you come on inside, Leanne,'' Jay

suggested. "I'm sure we've got some beer in the fridge and I can cook up a mean pot of chili con carne right from the can."

"No, that's all right. I've really got to get back to the lab. I've got a time-sensitive experiment going. I just wanted to see that everything was okay with my sister."

"Great. Drop by anytime," Jay said. "I'll leave you two alone and go wash off some of this sand I picked up at the beach."

As he walked up onto the porch, he brushed the back of his cutoffs with his hand.

"Nice buns," Leanne murmured appreciatively.

It was Kim's turn to raise her brows. "I didn't think you ever noticed men."

"Oh, I notice all right. It's just that they don't give me and my scrawny figure a second glance." When Jay vanished behind the closed door, she turned back to Kim. "Is he really blind? With those glasses, I didn't realize—"

"We're hoping it's temporary. He'll know in a few days."

"What a tragedy if he doesn't get his vision back. Are you and he serious?"

Kim wasn't sure how to answer Leanne's question. She was very serious about Jay; she'd lost her heart to him years ago. But that didn't mean they could make happily-ever-after come true or should even try. "Mother was appalled at the idea of me being involved with a firefighter."

"Maybe she just envies you. I know I do. He's

some kind of hunk.'' She moved down the walkway toward her car. ''Seems to me we've both spent a lot of years trying to please our parents.''

Kim trailed behind her. ''Something you've done more successfully than I have.''

''Maybe. But it hasn't always been easy. When the folks realized I was a genius, their expectations for me and my future shot through the roof. Not that I don't love my job, mind you. There are just a lot of things I wanted to try but never had the chance.'' Walking around to the driver's side of the car, she unlocked it. ''My gut feeling is you ought to please yourself and not worry about Mother. But let me know if you decide you don't want him.''

''Why?''

With a dazzling grin, Leanne said, ''A hunk like Jay is exactly what I've always wanted to try and never had the chance.''

Despite Kim's laughter, a quick stab of jealousy pierced her heart. Leanne had everything—brains, beauty she'd never had to utilize to get what she wanted and parental love. Kim damn well didn't want to hand Jay over to her sister on a silver platter.

But she wasn't sure she could keep him either. Not once he got a good look at her.

THE LONG-AWAITED phone call came the day of Jay's appointment to have his patches removed and his eyes checked.

As soon as Kim hung up, she launched herself into Jay's arms. ''That was Mr. Abbott. I got it, Jay.

KUCP. He wants me to start next week. Oh, God, I was so afraid—''

"The issue was never in doubt, sweetheart." He whirled her around the room in his arms. "We're going to have to celebrate big time tonight. You've got a job and I'm going to be able to see again."

"Yes, of course," she whispered, her fears vanquishing her excitement, dread bubbling to the surface and nearly choking her.

"You sound nervous."

"Maybe a little. But stage fright is a good thing. Makes you sharp." Although her anxiety had little to do with sitting in front of a microphone and more to do with seeing her image reflected in Jay's eyes.

Some time later, when they'd dressed for the doctor's appointment, Jay said, "So how do I look?"

"Very handsome, as always." His vertically striped polo shirt tucked in at the waist of his pants emphasized his broad chest and lean hips. His hair was neatly combed, his face clean-shaven. Except for the dark patches covering his eyes, he could easily have stepped right out of one of those men's casual-dress catalogues.

"I know that. But I don't want to open my eyes and find you switched all the clothes in my closet and I'm walking around in chartreuse pants and a purple shirt."

"Not likely," she said with a tight laugh.

He picked up his dark glasses from the end table and slipped them on, making Kim's image spin in the reflective lenses. "Then I'm ready to go. You'll be right there with me, won't you? Forget my chartreuse pants. You're the first thing I want to see when they take off these damn patches.''

Panic whipped through her, her courage faltering. "I'm, uh, not sure they'll let me into the examining room.''

"I don't see why not. But we'll find out when we get there.''

THE DOCTOR'S OFFICE was in a medical building near the hospital, a three-story glass and concrete structure. Kim cruised the lot until she found a spot to park. Jay took her arm and they went inside, riding the elevator to the top floor.

"Hard to believe that on the way back I'll be able to see where I'm going," Jay said. "God, I hope I don't fall all over my feet and break my neck. That'd be some kind of irony, wouldn't it?'' His anxiety radiated through her arm like an electric current.

"You'll be fine," she assured him, though she wasn't quite so confident about herself. And given his injuries, there was no guarantee he'd regain his sight. Fully restored vision was only one of a range of possibilities—the one she prayed for. Not for herself, but for him.

Still self-conscious about her scars when meeting new people, she adjusted her scarf before opening the office door.

Generic best described the decor—nondescript pictures on the walls, thinly padded chairs with straight arms and low backs, and a kiddie corner with a plastic basket filled with well-worn toys. A mother and a child about seven years old looked up as they entered. Kim led Jay to the chairs across from them.

"There's an empty chair a foot to your left. Sit down and I'll sign you in."

Thankfully, Jay did as she'd asked. At the window counter, she leaned in towards the receptionist. "Mr. Tolliver is feeling a little anxious about the procedure today," she whispered. "I think it might be better if I waited out here until after the examination is over." Perhaps the extra few minutes would give her nerves enough time to settle down and unclog her throat.

"Sure," the receptionist said. "Whatever he wants."

Kim nodded her thanks. "And if you'd let me know before I go in with him if he can, uh, see or not, I'd appreciate it."

The receptionist shrugged. "Whatever."

Kim took a seat next to Jay, picked up a magazine, flipped through it, then set it aside. No way could she concentrate on an article about the drug cartel in South America.

Jay's foot tapped double-time to the beat of the piped-in elevator music. "Nerves are good, right?"

She rested her hand on his arm, noting the way her fingers trembled. If there were a way to measure anxiety, both she and Jay would be off the Richter scale.

When the nurse called Jay, they both jumped.

"I'll wait here for you," Kim said. She needed to do this. Jay *needed* her. But she didn't want her scars to be the very first thing he saw, she told herself.

"No, I want you in the room—"

"It's better if she stays out here for now, Mr. Tolliver," the nurse said smoothly. "We'll call her when it's time."

Tears pressing against the backs of her eyes, Kim gave him a quick kiss. "Go with her, Jay. The nurse will show you the way."

The door to the inner sanctum swung shut with a solid click like the closing of a cell door. Both she and Jay were locked in a prison of fate's making through no fault of their own. In Jay's prison, his vision and his independence were at stake; Kim's jailers battered her already shaky self-esteem. Would either of them find a way to escape?

She picked up another magazine, flipped through the pages. Nothing of interest caught her eye.

"Why is that lady's face so ugly?" the child across from her said in a stage whisper loud enough that it would have reached to the far corners of Carnegie Hall.

Instinctively, her head snapped up. Embarrassed heat scorched her *ugly* face. *Oh, God...*

"Hush, Jimmy," his mother admonished. She gave Kim an apologetic look. "You're not supposed to say things like that."

"But it's tru—oo," the boy complained, pulling his face into a pout. "She's got—"

"I'm going to tan your hide if you don't hush this minute. Do you hear me, James Derby?"

"Please don't," Kim said, aghast that she'd be the cause of a child being spanked when he was only saying what other people thought and were too polite to say.

She *was* ugly. She'd confronted that reality in the mirror every day for months. Only with Jay had she ignored the truth, feeling beautiful again. A woman worthy of a man's love. Not a caricature of a clown.

When they removed Jay's patches—even if he retained only limited vision—he would see that truth, too. Dear God, she couldn't bear that.

"I'VE DIMMED the lights," the doctor said as Jay sat rigidly in the examination chair. "When I remove the dressing, I want you to open your eyes slowly. It will take a little while for your eyes to adjust to the light. Then I want you to tell me what you see."

Jay closed his hands around the ends of the armrests. His mouth was as dry as the Sahara, his heart hammering like a loose cylinder in his chest. God, he wished Kim were here. He needed to hold on to her.

In desperation, he conjured up an image of her in high school, tossing her blond hair away from her face as she flirted with one of the jocks that crowded around her. Her eyes sparkled like the sun slanting off the lupines in spring, turning the hillsides a vibrant blue so deep it was almost purple. Her radiant smile lit up the room.

Why hadn't he tried to get to know her better then? Somewhere he could have found the time and money to take her out, at least for a cola. Why had he waited so long just dreaming of her?

Because he'd never felt worthy of her.

The doctor peeled back the gauze. Jay's eye lids remained stuck together as if they'd been glued that way—or maybe he was too damn scared to open them. The doctor daubed something that was cold and smelled of antiseptic on his closed eyelids.

"That ought to do it," the doctor assured him. "Open slowly now."

With a force of will, Jay commanded his eyelids to open. Light! Bright! Painfully penetrating. He squinted his eyes closed again.

"You saw something?" the doctor asked.

"It's awful bright in here, Doc."

"Try it again. Keep your eyes open a little longer this time."

Jay did as ordered. Shapes began to form. The doctor's silhouette sitting in front of him. Eye-testing machinery to Jay's left, a red light glowing on the wall behind the counter to his right.

A combination of excitement, hope and relief rose in him like a tidal surge. "I can see shapes."

"That's good. Let's try with a little more light."

Jay squinted again as the doctor brought up the lights, but slowly, details came into focus. The doctor was younger than he had thought and wore a tidy beard and mustache. The small room was shaped like a truncated slice of pie with the reading chart at the narrow end. Even in the shadows he could make out the first three rows of letters. A nurse who'd been in and out of the room a couple of times was standing by the door.

"Can we get my girlfriend in here now? I want to—"

"We have a little testing to do first, and then she can come in. It will only take a few minutes."

The nurse opened the door to the hallway, admitting a stunning column of light, then closed it behind her.

IN A PANIC, Kim rose to her feet. The nurse who had escorted Jay to the back room was by the receptionist.

"Nurse? Mr. Tolliver—has the doctor removed his patches yet?"

"Yes." The young woman in white beamed her smile. "His vision seems quite good. Mr. Tolliver is anxious to see you, but the doctor has a few more tests to run."

Kim exhaled in relief for Jay. He would be able to see. He wouldn't need anyone to lead him around, drive him where he wanted to go. He'd no longer need her.

She looked around the office for a frantic moment, seeking some way of escape. A way to avoid Jay seeing her. It might be cowardly to leave when she'd promised to stay. Cold. Unfeeling. But she simply couldn't stay when she knew exactly what she'd see in Jay's eyes the first time he looked at her.

That she was ugly, a woman to be pitied.

"Excuse me," she said to the receptionist. Guilt and regret mixed into a knot in Kim's stomach. "When Mr. Tolliver completes his examination, could you tell him I was called away? Something about my new job," she ad-libbed. "And then could you call him a cab?"

"Sure, if you want." The receptionist looked at her curiously. "Say, do I know you from somewhere?"

"No, I don't think so." The woman the receptionist recognized had vanished amid the rubble left by the earthquake. Kim was an entirely different person now. An *ugly,* cowardly woman who didn't deserve to be loved by a man like Jay.

JAY'S REMAINING TESTS took an eternity, or so it seemed to him. His eyes were measured in every conceivable way and the verdict was all Jay had hoped for.

"You're a fortunate man," the doctor said as he slid the examining equipment out of Jay's way. "Your retinas are completely intact, no scarring that I can observe and your vision is back to twenty-twenty. You'll want to wear dark glasses for a couple of days while your eyes get fully accustomed to the light again. Other than that, I recommend you not give away your helmet next time."

"Yes, sir. What about work? When can I go back on the job?"

"I'd give it a couple of days. Next week should be fine."

Jay wanted to leap up in the air and click his heels together. Or swing Tarzan-style from the training tower. But most of all, he wanted to see Kim.

"Can I go now?" he asked.

The doctor nodded. "Check with my receptionist.

Just to be sure, I'll want a follow-up appointment in three months. In the meantime, if you have any problems at all, call me.''

''Got it.''

Outside the examining room, Jay discovered he was oddly disoriented, not knowing whether to turn left or right to reach the front desk. The hallway, the smiling nurses, all looked unfamiliar. He had to close his eyes before he could remember which way he'd come in from the waiting area.

The receptionist was talking with someone on the phone. Jay peered past her counter to the waiting patients, looking for Kim, but she wasn't in sight. He thought they'd been sitting across from the receptionist. Maybe he was wrong.

When the receptionist was free, he made an appointment for his next visit. The thrill of seeing Kim for the first time since the earthquake had him rattled, and he couldn't remember C shift's schedule. He'd call back to make a change if necessary.

Anticipation turned his stomach to knots as he opened the door to the waiting area. Everyone looked up expectantly. He scanned the room for Kim's familiar smile, her distinctive blue eyes. He'd take her to a classy place tonight, a fancy dinner and some dancing at the beach. They both had a lot to celebrate.

Slowly his brain acknowledged she wasn't there. Only an elderly couple and a man in a business suit. Anticipation turned to dread.

''Miss,'' he said to the receptionist. ''The woman

I came in with—did she have to go down the hall or something?''

The woman looked at him blankly for a moment. ''Oh, I'm sorry. I forgot to tell you. Your friend had to leave. She said it was something about her job, and she asked me to call you a cab.''

A cab? Despair nearly drove Jay to his knees. She'd left. Walked out on him at one of the best moments of his life. Nothing about her job should have been that important.

Why, dammit? He wanted to know why she'd left him high and dry.

Chapter Fourteen

She didn't return his phone calls at the radio station. Her home phone was unlisted, and he didn't know where the hell she lived, except it was up in the hills east of town. He'd been there, and he still didn't know where he'd been.

Granted, he knew if he asked Chief Gray, his boss would probably tell him where to find Kim. But he couldn't embarrass himself further by letting anyone know he'd lost the woman he loved.

Jay lay on his back in his room at the fire station, staring up at the acoustic-tile ceiling counting the holes in the tiles, listening to Kim's voice come to him courtesy of KUCP. He was aroused and hoped to God they didn't have to roll to a fire. He'd probably injure an important part of his anatomy if he had to slide down the pole any time soon.

A month ago she'd been in his arms. Now all he had was the bluesy sound of her voice and his memories.

Cursing, he rolled to his side. What good was perfect vision if you couldn't see the person you loved?

He could only assume Kim had concluded she'd done her good deed—she'd rescued him from the clutches of his own foolishness when he was blind. Now that she'd done her duty, returned the favor, she was outta here. What woman with her looks and charisma would settle for a simple firefighter who liked scuba diving and rock climbing. Hell, she was a real intellectual. Who knew or cared about Saddam Hussein?

Except Kim did.

Pounding his pillow with his fist, Jay listened as she segued into her next segment, introducing the topic of El Niño's threat to the coastal beaches of central California. Her guest was a marine geologist from the university.

Boring. All Jay wanted to do was listen to Kim's voice and remember the day they'd walked along the beach together. Amazingly, he was just getting into the topic, worried about beach erosion, when the fire tone sounded. He was on his feet, adrenaline pumping and into his turnout pants and coat in seconds. Still, he was the last man down the pole. At least all of his important body parts were still intact.

An hour later they were mopping up after a suspicious carport fire, one of many they'd had lately in the area. Both Mike Gables and he were shoving push brooms down the alley.

"Have I mentioned it's sure good to have you back on the job?" Gables asked.

"A couple of times. I gather your love life is improving since you're not pulling so many double shifts?''

''Only a cad would kiss 'n' tell.''

''Right.'' Jay shoved a heap of debris away from the gutter.

''Speaking of love life, I haven't seen Kim around lately.''

''You're not likely to, either. She dumped me.'' Pure and simple, that's what had happened. But the admission hurt.

''You're kidding! Why would she do a damn fool thing like that?''

He shot his buddy a glance. ''You're the only guy I know who has women knocking on his door day and night. You tell me.''

''Hell, I haven't figured women out yet, I'm not even sure I want to.'' Leaning on his broom, he appeared to study the pile of burned rubble with exceptional interest. ''I do know, the look I saw in Kim's eyes when you were in the room would have sent me running in the opposite direction as fast as my legs could carry me.''

Jay paused the stroke of his broom in mid sweep. ''Why is that?''

''She was in love, man. Thinking about happily ever after. That scares the hell out of me.''

Mike had it all wrong. Jay was sure of that. If Kim had been in love with him, she wouldn't have walked away. It wouldn't have made any sense.

It didn't matter that Jay loved her. Maybe it was just as well he'd never told her. No chance of her feeling guilty about him as she got on with her life and her new career.

MR. ABBOTT caught Kim in the hallway before she went on the air. "Do you have a minute?" he asked.

"Of course." Surprised to see him at the station so late in the evening, she wondered if last night's segment when she'd interviewed prominent doctors about euthanasia had hit a sour chord with the public. She'd had a lot of callers, all with very strong feelings on the subject. In fact, every evening and on into the morning the number of callers had increased.

But none of the callers had been Jay. He'd quit calling the station after the first week. She couldn't blame him. After all, she hadn't returned his calls. She'd been too much of a coward. He had every right in the world to give up on her.

Dear heaven, she missed him. Despite her new job, every waking minute she thought about him. When she finally fell asleep, he crept into her dreams, too. Meanwhile, she'd lost ten pounds because food didn't interest her, and she was actually looking gaunt—as her mother had ungraciously pointed out.

Mr. Abbott ushered her into his office and closed the door. A dapper man in his sixties, his expertise lay more in the arena of fund-raising than broadcasting.

"I have good news for you and bad news for KUCP," he said.

Kim waited to hear if she'd crossed some unseen line in the broadcasting business.

"Your reputation for lively discussions and interesting guests has apparently spread across the country. The network CEO called me this afternoon. They're interested in syndicating 'Late Night with Lydell' for public radio. You'd probably be picked up by two or three hundred stations."

Kim's legs threatened to buckle and she sat down in the chair in front of Mr. Abbott's desk. "Me? They want me for a network show?" She'd given up her dream of being on a network months ago. Granted, public radio wasn't what she'd had in mind, but the network carried its own special, well-respected status in the industry.

"There is a small hitch," Mr. Abbott continued. "They want you to be based in either New York or Washington, D.C. They feel you'd be better able to access guests with an international reputation from there than from our small town."

Her budding excitement tumbled. She'd have to leave Paseo del Real. Leave Jay.

Even though she didn't see him, his presence in her unseen audience gave her comfort. She talked to *him*, not to faceless listeners. He was in the room with her, in her heart, whenever she went on the air. That's why her show had been so successful, the sense of intimacy she brought to the programs.

How could she possibly do that from New York?

Yet how could she turn down the opportunity? If not quite all that she'd dreamed about, a regular spot on national public radio came close.

A quick glance at the clock on Mr. Abbott's desk

reminded Kim she'd be on the air in a few minutes. She had to get to the studio and set up for her live interviews.

Standing, she said, "May I have a few days to think about the offer?"

"Of course, but don't wait too long. When the network execs make a decision, they don't like to be kept waiting."

"I understand." She had this one chance. If she didn't take it now the opportunity might never come again.

Excusing herself, she hurried down the hall to the studio. Her mind was a jumble of conflicting emotions. Although she had lived in other towns as she was building her television career, this was different. In many ways she'd be severing her ties with Paseo del Real—and with Jay. Moving on without him.

Would he care? Or had he recovered from her cowardly act of leaving him at the doctor's office and moved on with his own life? She'd been such a fool. No matter that she was ugly or that they had little in common. She should have taken the risk, given them both a chance to find happiness.

For the next two days, she vacillated over her decision. Finally she decided to pose the question to her listeners, one in particular if he was still tuned in.

"Good evening, Paseo del Real," she said at the opening of the show. "This is 'Late Night with Lydell' and I'm Kimberly Lydell, your host. Tonight I have a personal question for you. I have an opportunity to have my own show on national public radio.

The one glitch is that I'd have to move back east, and that's a long way from Paseo del Real." *And the man I love.*

"What I want you to do, late-night listeners, is call in. I want you to talk me into taking the job…or into staying right here in Paseo." Knowing there would be only one vote that truly counted, she gave the listeners the station call-in number.

Joe, on the other side of the glass partition in the control booth, gave her a thumbs-up, and they cut to taped public-service announcements.

Almost immediately her phone lines lit up. Kim could only hope one of the callers was Jay giving her a reason to stay.

AFTER MIDNIGHT, with Kim's program playing quietly on the radio, the door to Jay's room at the fire station burst open. In walked Mrs. Anderson, her hair unkempt, her eyes wild, as though she'd just awakened from a bad dream.

Wearing his usual sleeping attire of briefs and a T-shirt, Jay scrambled to cover himself. "Ma'am, I don't think you should be here." At least she hadn't brought with her the potent smell of lilacs, a scent so strong he'd never be able to get it out of his room.

"Nonsense, I'm a city councilwoman and this is city property. I can be anywhere I like."

Jay grabbed for a pair of trousers and pulled them on. "Ma'am, I really don't think—"

"You've been listening to her, haven't you?" She

pointed to the radio that was still tuned to Kim's show.

"Yeah." He'd heard Kim announce she'd landed a network job—her dream. She'd be moving away. This call-in business she'd set up asking people to talk her out of going was probably because some guest hadn't shown up. She was filling air time. All during the show, Jay hadn't been able to draw a decent breath. He'd lost her forever.

Mrs. Anderson planted her fists on her hips. "So what are you going to do about Kim leaving, young man?"

"I can't stop her."

"Of course you can, and you're going to. I didn't go out of my way to help get her that job at KUCP only to have her pack up and leave the first time something better comes along. We need people like Kimberly Lydell in our town." She scowled as if considering retracting that statement. "Even if she is a closet liberal."

"Ma'am, I don't really think it's any of your—"

"My business is seeing to the welfare of this community. I want you to get on the phone and give her one good reason to stay right here in Paseo."

"If she doesn't want to stay, there wouldn't be enough reasons in the world to—"

"You love her, don't you?"

By now the rest of the men on C shift had gathered around his door taking in the scene the councilwoman was creating. He wasn't going to make a fool of himself in front of all of his friends.

"He loves her, all right," Gables volunteered. "He's been moping around the station for weeks. He's been losing weight—"

"Am not."

"—and he's become such a grouch, not even Buttons can stand being around him."

Mrs. Anderson pulled herself up into an aristocratic pose. "Then you must call that woman and put her out of her misery. Tell her you love her."

"That's not something a man can say over the phone." Not that he'd had a chance to tell Kim anything since she wouldn't return his calls. "And I can't exactly walk off the job to have a little social tête-à-tête."

"Okay, fellow smoke eaters, here's what we're gonna do." Gables took the lead, insisting they roll Engine 61 with the whole crew on board just like a trip to the grocery store when it was their turn to fix the shift's chow. Only this time they'd go to the TV station. Jay could tell Kim how he felt in person.

Jay's protests fell on deaf ears.

Clutching the cell phone the councilwoman had pressed into his hand at the last minute, Jay climbed into his seat behind the driver. If Kim turned him down—or even if she didn't—he'd be making a fool of himself in front of all his friends. But maybe, just maybe, it would be worth it.

THE HANDS on the studio clock moved relentlessly toward the closing moments of the show. Kim had been amazed at the number of people who had called asking her to stay in Paseo, that this was the best place on earth to live. Even her sister had called reminding her that families should stick together, a notion that had brought tears to Kim's eyes.

But no one had given her the one convincing reason to stay she wouldn't be able to resist.

Jay hadn't called.

She was about to wrap up the show when the phone light went on again. One last call. It would have to be a quicky.

She threw the switch on the two-second delay for the phone, lest the airwaves be filled with foul language, and spoke into the mike. ''This is 'Late Night with Lydell.' Are you voting I should stay or go?''

There was a pause on the other end of the crackling line.

''Hello?'' she said. Great time for a prank caller, she mentally muttered.

''It's me, Kim.''

Her breathing stalled. ''Jay?''

''Who did you expect, blue eyes?''

''I thought—''

''You left in kind of a hurry last time.''

''I'm sorry.'' Her eyes filled with guilty tears. ''I was afraid—''

''Answer me this, if you can. Do you love me?''

Her tongue tangled with itself. ''Yes,'' she whispered. ''But I was afraid when you saw me—''

''You're beautiful. I told you before I love the way that sweater matches your eyes. And the pearls. Sexy.''

"How did you—" She glanced up and saw him standing in the control booth, his turnout coat hanging open as if he'd just come from a fire. Jay was looking right at her, talking to her on a cell phone. Seeing her scars for the first time. Instinctively she wanted to duck away, to hide herself, but she was mesmerized by the look in his deep brown eyes.

"I want you to stay, Kim. I love you and I want to marry you."

Every atom in Kim's body went still. She didn't breathe. Her blood stopped flowing and her heart seized.

That's what she saw in his eyes. Not pity. Not horror at the ugly mask her face had become. *Love.*

Joe frantically signalled from the control booth for her to do something about the dead air. To talk. To say anything. But words wouldn't come to her. She had a live mike in front of her and she couldn't utter a single sound. All she could do was experience the cataclysmic emotions that shook her as she gazed into Jay's loving eyes.

And the whole town had just heard Jay's proposal. They deserved an answer, and so did Jay.

"Yes, I'll marry you." Her voice was so husky she wasn't sure the words carried to the mike much less to Jay's heart. But his smile told her he'd heard her loud and clear. And then she simply stared at Jay, her heart so full it filled her throat and she wasn't sure she'd ever be able to speak again.

Leaning forward and grinning, Joe switched on his own mike. "That's it for 'Late Night with Lydell,' folks. This is KUCP bringing you music till dawn.

My guess is Ms. Lydell is planning to stay in Paseo for a long, long time.''

The phone lines on Kim's console lit up one after another. She ignored them.

Standing, she met Jay as he came into the broadcast booth. His copper-brown eyes assessed her.

"Why did you leave the doctor's office?" he asked.

"I was afraid of what I'd see in your eyes. I didn't want your pity.''

"And what do you see there now, blue eyes?" Like the deep timbre of his voice, husky with emotion, his gaze caressed her.

"Love. You really do love me, don't you?"

"It's not something a man lies about, particularly when the news is being broadcast all over central California.''

Her heart jump-started. "We don't have much in common," she pointed out.

"I'm taking an art-appreciation class at the junior college. I can even tell the difference between French impressionists and modernists now. And I got that book from the library on Hussein that you mentioned. He's quite a character.''

"Oh, Jay." She pressed her palm to his chest, cherishing the rapid beat of his heart, the warmth of his flesh beneath his T-shirt. He'd been trying so hard to please her and she hadn't even known. She'd been too afraid to give him a chance—give *them* a chance. "I asked that marine geologist I had on the show to take me snorkeling. Once I got over my initial fear, I loved it.''

"I'll teach you to scuba dive. We could go to the Caribbean for our honeymoon."

"I'll never be able to rock climb, though. I don't have enough arm strength."

"It doesn't matter. There's only room for one tough guy in a family anyway. I love you, Kim. Just as you are, beautiful and sexy in every way." He ran his fingertips lightly over her scars, letting her know he still found her beautiful.

Happiness nearly overwhelmed her as she stepped into his embrace.

"If you want that network job, we can move to New York or wherever you need to be," he said. "I don't want you to lose your dream because of me."

"You *are* my dream, Jay Tolliver. You have been for a very long time. I love you and I'll be happy to go on loving you right here in Paseo."

Dipping his head, he caught her mouth in a fierce kiss that told her all she needed to know. He loved her and would until there wasn't a breath left in him. As she would love him in return with her very last ounce of strength. Forever.

* * * * *

Don't miss
WITH VALOR AND DEVOTION,
the next book in
the MEN OF STATION SIX *miniseries,*
coming next month
from Charlotte Maclay and
Harlequin American Romance.

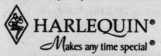

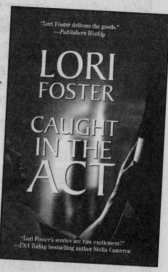

Harlequin truly does make any time special.... This year we are celebrating weddings in style!

To help us celebrate, we want you to tell us how wearing the Harlequin wedding gown will make your wedding day special. As the grand prize, Harlequin will offer one lucky bride the chance to **"Walk Down the Aisle"** in the Harlequin wedding gown!

There's more...

For her honeymoon, she and her groom will spend five nights at the **Hyatt Regency Maui.** As part of this five-night honeymoon at the hotel renowned for its romantic attractions, the couple will enjoy a candlelit dinner for two in Swan Court, a sunset sail on the hotel's catamaran, and duet spa treatments.

Maui • Molokai • Lanai

To enter, please write, in, 250 words or less, how wearing the Harlequin wedding gown will make your wedding day special. The entry will be judged based on its emotionally compelling nature, its originality and creativity, and its sincerity. This contest is open to Canadian and U.S. residents only and to those who are 18 years of age and older. There is no purchase necessary to enter. Void where prohibited. See further contest rules attached. Please send your entry to:

Walk Down the Aisle Contest

In Canada
P.O. Box 637
Fort Erie, Ontario
L2A 5X3

In U.S.A.
P.O. Box 9076
3010 Walden Ave.
Buffalo, NY 14269-9076

You can also enter by visiting www.eHarlequin.com
Win the Harlequin wedding gown and the vacation of a lifetime!
The deadline for entries is October 1, 2001.

HARLEQUIN®
Makes any time special ®

PHWDACONT1

1. To enter, follow directions published in the offer to which you are responding. Contest begins April 2, 2001, and ends on October 1, 2001. Method of entry may vary. Mailed entries must be postmarked by October 1, 2001, and received by October 8, 2001.

2. Contest entry may be, at times, presented via the Internet, but will be restricted solely to residents of certain geographic areas that are disclosed on the Web site. To enter via the Internet, if permissible, access the Harlequin Web site (www.eHarlequin.com) and follow the directions displayed online. Online entries must be received by 11:59 p.m. E.S.T. on October 1, 2001.

   In lieu of submitting an entry online, enter by mail by hand-printing (or typing) on an 8½" x 11" plain piece of paper, your name, address (including zip code), Contest number/name and in 250 words or fewer, why winning a Harlequin wedding dress would make your wedding day special. Mail via first-class mail to: Harlequin Walk Down the Aisle Contest 1197, (in the U.S.) P.O. Box 9076, 3010 Walden Avenue, Buffalo, NY 14269-9076, (in Canada) P.O. Box 637, Fort Erie, Ontario L2A 5X3, Canada.

   Limit one entry per person, household address and e-mail address. Online and/or mailed entries received from persons residing in geographic areas in which Internet entry is not permissible will be disqualified.

3. Contests will be judged by a panel of members of the Harlequin editorial, marketing and public relations staff based on the following criteria:

   - Originality and Creativity—50%
   - Emotionally Compelling—25%
   - Sincerity—25%

   In the event of a tie, duplicate prizes will be awarded. Decisions of the judges are final.

4. All entries become the property of Torstar Corp. and will not be returned. No responsibility is assumed for lost, late, illegible, incomplete, inaccurate, nondelivered or misdirected mail or misdirected e-mail, for technical, hardware or software failures of any kind, lost or unavailable network connections, or failed, incomplete, garbled or delayed computer transmission or any human error which may occur in the receipt or processing of the entries in this Contest.

5. Contest open only to residents of the U.S. (except Puerto Rico) and Canada, who are 18 years of age or older, and is void wherever prohibited by law; all applicable laws and regulations apply. Any litigation within the Province of Quebec respecting the conduct or organization of a publicity contest may be submitted to the Régie des alcools, des courses et des jeux for a ruling. Any litigation respecting the awarding of a prize may be submitted to the Régie des alcools, des courses et des jeux only for the purpose of helping the parties reach a settlement. Employees and immediate family members of Torstar Corp. and D. L. Blair, Inc., their affiliates, subsidiaries and all other agencies, entities and persons connected with the use, marketing or conduct of this Contest are not eligible to enter. Taxes on prizes are the sole responsibility of winners. Acceptance of any prize offered constitutes permission to use winner's name, photograph or other likeness for the purposes of advertising, trade and promotion on behalf of Torstar Corp., its affiliates and subsidiaries without further compensation to the winner, unless prohibited by law.

6. Winners will be determined no later than November 15, 2001, and will be notified by mail. Winners will be required to sign and return an Affidavit of Eligibility form within 15 days after winner notification. Noncompliance within that time period may result in disqualification and an alternative winner may be selected. Winners of trip must execute a Release of Liability prior to ticketing and must possess required travel documents (e.g. passport, photo ID) where applicable. Trip must be completed by November 2002. No substitution of prize permitted by winner. Torstar Corp. and D. L. Blair, Inc., their parents, affiliates, and subsidiaries are not responsible for errors in printing or electronic presentation of Contest, entries and/or game pieces. In the event of printing or other errors which may result in unintended prize values or duplication of prizes, all affected game pieces or entries shall be null and void. If for any reason the Internet portion of the Contest is not capable of running as planned, including infection by computer virus, bugs, tampering, unauthorized intervention, fraud, technical failures, or any other causes beyond the control of Torstar Corp. which corrupt or affect the administration, secrecy, fairness, integrity or proper conduct of the Contest, Torstar Corp. reserves the right, at its sole discretion, to disqualify any individual who tampers with the entry process and to cancel, terminate, modify or suspend the Contest or the Internet portion thereof. In the event of a dispute regarding an online entry, the entry will be deemed submitted by the authorized holder of the e-mail account submitted at the time of entry. Authorized account holder is defined as the natural person who is assigned to an e-mail address by an Internet access provider, online service provider or other organization that is responsible for arranging e-mail address for the domain associated with the submitted e-mail address. **Purchase or acceptance of a product offer does not improve your chances of winning.**

7. Prizes: (1) Grand Prize—A Harlequin wedding dress (approximate retail value: $3,500) and a 5-night/6-day honeymoon trip to Maui, HI, including round-trip air transportation provided by Maui Visitors Bureau from Los Angeles International Airport (winner is responsible for transportation to and from Los Angeles International Airport) and a Harlequin Romance Package, including hotel accomodations (double occupancy) at the Hyatt Regency Maui Resort and Spa, dinner for (2) two at Swan Court, a sunset sail on Kiele V and a spa treatment for the winner (approximate retail value: $4,000); (5) Five runner-up prizes of a $1000 gift certificate to selected retail outlets to be determined by Sponsor (retail value $1000 ea.). Prizes consist of only those items listed as part of the prize. Limit one prize per person. All prizes are valued in U.S. currency.

8. For a list of winners (available after December 17, 2001) send a self-addressed, stamped envelope to: Harlequin Walk Down the Aisle Contest 1197 Winners, P.O. Box 4200 Blair, NE 68009-4200 or you may access the www.eHarlequin.com Web site through January 15, 2002.

Contest sponsored by Torstar Corp., P.O. Box 9042, Buffalo, NY 14269-9042, U.S.A.

PHWDACONT2

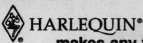

COMING SOON...

AN EXCITING
OPPORTUNITY TO SAVE
ON THE PURCHASE OF
HARLEQUIN AND
SILHOUETTE BOOKS!

*DETAILS TO FOLLOW
IN OCTOBER 2001!*

YOU WON'T WANT TO MISS IT!

PHQ401

HARLEQUIN®
Makes any time special®

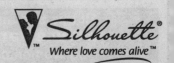

Silhouette®
Where love comes alive™

If you enjoyed what you just read,
then we've got an offer you can't resist!

Take 2 bestselling love stories FREE!

Plus get a FREE surprise gift!